WINNER TAKES ALL

A Harlow Mystery

Claris Lam

ISBN-13 (ebook): 978-1-7781998-1-3
ISBN-13 (physical): 978-1-7781998-8-2
ISBN-10: 1477123456

Cover design by: Claris Lam
Library of Congress Control Number: 2018675309
Printed in the United States of America

CONTENTS

CHAPTER 1

Aubri felt a breath leave her lungs as she got off the small plane and looked up at the huge resort at the top of the hill several feet ahead of her, before inhaling the scent of the salty sea from the fresh ocean waves. Her shoulders relaxed as she exhaled, gazing at the dream-like, sunny skies.

This wasn't a dream – it was real, and she knew she'd get to bask in this sight after winning that free-vacation contest only a few weeks ago.

As she approached the stairs leading up to the resort entrance, she noticed a nearby sign reading "The Calloway Island Resort." Going up the hill and closer to the resort entrance, she noticed that the luxurious-looking wooden stairs were steep. The surrounding beaches, with silvery-gold sand, glimmered in the afternoon sunlight.

She usually didn't go to expensive resorts such as this one. She didn't have the money to afford something like this. However, *winning* a free trip was a whole other thing. It was her first vacation since graduating high school, and she never took a day off during her university years.

Aubri didn't deny that she was a workaholic. At least here, on the island, she didn't have to worry about pouring late nights into work. She didn't have to worry about people pestering her about dating, either. She could just relax and take it all in for herself, for once, without worrying about what anyone thought of her or dealing with lingering ties.

As she made her way even closer to the resort's main entrance, and towards the main building to check in, she recalled reading about the resort after she won the contest. As the winner, she didn't have to pay for the seven nights she'd stay at this place as advertised, nor did she have to pay for the private, first-class plane provided for the way there and back. Sure, she'd have to pay for room service and other extra amenities, like the spa, but the wi-fi was free, the large pool in the hotel area was crystal clear and ready to swim in, and the entire area looked something out of a romance novel; scenic, gorgeous, and spotless.

It would be a great setting for a murder mystery, too. Aubri could easily count the many mysteries she read, many of them taking place at hotels or resorts – especially ones as fancy as this. A lot of murders seemed to happen in hotel rooms too, for some strange reason, especially the locked-door mysteries. It was a common trend in most mystery novels she read, she didn't mind reading. It made things more exciting, trying to imagine herself in that scenario. Not that she wanted an actual murder to happen in real life, of course, but it was nice to at least imagine it.

Also, the winner's room was a whole big suite all for herself, fully furnished. She didn't know what to expect of the room, despite doing her best to check out the interior previews of the room online beforehand, she hoped it was as good as they claimed. That would certainly be something to take a few selfies in.

As she made her way up the steps leading up to the resort's main entrance, to check in, she noticed someone standing in front of the building ahead of her. He wore a plain, button-up white shirt, with a familiar, grey blazer embroidered with a lily at the breast pocket, and matching-coloured slacks. Black, fine shoes finished off the look, and as he looked up from his phone to see her, Aubri swallowed, pushing a few strands of light brown hair out of her own face.

She knew who this person was – and he was one of the last people she ever expected to see here.

"Aubri?" He stared at her, brows furrowing. Despite it being a few years since she last saw him, his short dark brown hair, silvering at the roots if one looked closely enough, was unmistakable. His eyes, a lighter shade of brown compared to his hair, gazed right at her with familiarity and surprise. "Is that you?"

Had anyone walked in on the two of them talking, right now, Aubri wasn't sure what they would think of it. An older man, younger woman…Aubri knew she was just *barely* too old for anyone passing by to assume she was Bastian's daughter.

"Yeah." Aubri, despite not wanting to, looked him in the eye. She offered him a soft smile, shrugging a little as she approached him – there was no point in hiding from him now that he noticed her after all. Despite the jitters in her chest, she tried to stay calm. "Sorry that I didn't keep in touch."

"I don't blame you for ghosting me, given all that happened." Bastian shrugged, smoothing back his noticeably greying hair. "I don't think either of us expected to see each other again, after all."

"Agreed." She paused, then asked, "So, um, why are you here? Just vacationing?"

"You could say that." A chuckle left him, and she recognized the excited sparkle in his eyes as he smiled. Even if he had been her ex-fake-boyfriend, she knew that he still had his charms after all this time. "I won a contest, and it's a seven-night stay here."

"Really?" She resisted the urge to drop her jaw at the news, but her eyes widened as she blurted out, "I won a contest for that exact same prize!"

"What?" He stared at her with raised brows. "Is it the same…wait." He quickly looked down at his phone, before showing her the ad on it. "Is it the same as *this* one?"

She nodded quickly, recognizing the ad immediately. The resort's logo, as well as the wording of the ad (*"Tell us what you want to do at Calloway, tag a friend, and you might win a 7-night stay!"*) was too familiar to her now. "Yup. That's the same contest."

"Well, it *did* mention it would pick a few winners…" He mused, putting his phone away, pushing a few strands of hair out of his face. "We're probably two of them."

"Two of them?" Aubri frowned. She hadn't paid too much attention to the fine details – were there more on the way here? "How many winners were they choosing, exactly? I didn't pay much attention to reading that part of the rules."

A soft hum left him, and he shrugged. "I think the actual website indicated *four* winners…so there's probably two more of us on the way here or they already just got here."

"I see." She figured, at this point, that she could live with Bastian being on the same island as her. It could always be worse, after all. She glanced toward the front doors, then toward him with a soft smile. "Well, I guess I'll be seeing you around?"

"Yeah." He nodded, averting his gaze from her briefly, but then he glanced back toward her with a smile. "See you around." He paused, before he looked towards the front door, opening it for her. "Want to head in?" He smiled. "Ladies first."

She chuckled, nodding. "Thank you. Still a gentleman like old times, I see." Even if the fake dates back then were, well, fake, they were still a good time.

A chuckle left him in return. "I strive to be, Aubri."

The most she and Bastian ever did was hug and hold hands, back in university. He just needed someone to have company with, mainly to chase off an obsessive woman who failed to understand that he was gay and would never be interested in her. Aubri and Bastian were classmates, and she trusted him, willing to help him out at the time. Also, Bastian was willing to *pay* her for her time, after she previously ranted to him several times, before or after class, about struggling to find a part-time job to pay down her student debt. The plan worked; Aubri got more money to pay her bills, and Bastian successfully deterred said ex from going after him after about a year of Aubri pretending to be his girlfriend.

Aubri was fine keeping this a secret from Colin, her then-boyfriend, now ex, at the time. She didn't think Colin would care about her fake-dating, to help a friend, so she never brought it up to him. He hadn't noticed at the time, either, given how inattentive he was.

She and Bastian hadn't talked since that whole faking-dating time, even though they amicably parted ways at the time. It wasn't like she hated him, but...she feared things getting awkward between her and Bastian, given all that previously happened with them and Colin. And now here she was, seeing him again. Funny, how fate brought them back together.

Aubri walked straight through the open door, making it fully in to stare up at the large fountain that made up the centre of the lobby. The waters flowing from it were crystal clear, sparkling in the sunlight shining down from the glass ceiling above, and the fountain itself was adorned with various blue gems. She wondered if the gems were real, or if they were just incredibly good replacements. She had a feeling it was the former, but they looked lovely, nonetheless. She briefly imagined a jewel thief sneaking through the hotel at the dead of night, just so he could steal the jewels in that fountain alone. If they were real, after all, they would be worth millions. Heists were a common trend in mystery novels too, right? It was hard not to imagine a scenario like this.

Checking in was fast and easy enough. She realized, as she received her keys from the front desk, that her room was located on the top floor. She watched Bastian check in next at the front desk as she entered the elevator, just before the elevator doors closed and started going up the several floors. There were *seven* floors to this hotel if she remembered correctly.

Aubri looked around the elevator as she waited. There was a touchscreen within the elevator, briefly showing off a map of the hotel before revealing several ads for the various activities available, the main dining area, and even the large pool. The upper left corner of the touchscreen displayed the various floors the elevator reached as it continued ascending. She was getting close to the seventh floor. Aubri couldn't stop the relieved breath leaving her lips; she just wanted to check out her room, settle in a bit, and avoid Bastian. At *least* he was still nice and held no hard feelings about her dropping all contact with him. That sudden reunion didn't go as badly as she thought. Despite that, however, she couldn't stop the odd, swishing feeling in her gut, twisting into knots.

As the elevator dinged, the doors opening to reveal floor seven, Aubri stepped out. There were four doors, two on each side of the wide hallway ahead of her, and she inspected the first two *(701* and *702)*, before checking her keys *(703)*. One of the doors further down had to be her room. As she took a few steps down the hallway, the door to her left opened, a dark-haired woman stepping out...who happened to be another familiar face. Aubri tried to avoid gazes with her, but it was too late as she heard her speak.

"Aubri?" Her voice was too familiar, warm, and honeyed, and Aubri couldn't help but shiver. "Is that *you?*"

CHAPTER 2

This resort was *not* where Aubri wanted to see her ex-girlfriend Renee, of all places. It was awkward enough seeing Bastian, earlier, even if they were still friendly, but seeing an ex was a whole other situation. However, she also knew she couldn't just ignore her, either. Taking a deep breath, she turned on her heel to fully face Renee, readying herself for the awkward consequences.

Renee looked like she grew an inch since Aubri last saw her (Renee's growth spurt was a little late compared to most people in their grade, back in high school). The lavender streaks she had in her blackish-brown hair perfectly framed her face. Brown, earthy eyes gazed into Aubri's own as if trying to see something else deep within her, rather than just maintaining contact.

"Renee." Aubri finally managed, trying not to shiver at how Renee gazed at her. "Hi. I, uh," She gestured to the doors around them, then to her, "I guess you won the contest, too?"

"Yeah, I did." Renee offered her a soft, but awkward smile, stepping forward. Aubri found herself rooted in the same spot where she stood, despite wanting to step back. "It's been a while, hasn't it? How's uni treated you?"

"Well," Aubri shrugged, hoping to that she could finish this small talk sooner than later, "You know how it is. Stress, grades, exams…"

"Ugh, *exams.*" A soft laugh escaped the other. "Those were a bummer."

"How'd your internship work out?" Aubri felt her chest

twinge as she asked that question, but she felt that she needed to know. It was what caused them to break up, after all.

Aubri knew it was her own fault for not wanting to stay together, despite Renee's insistence on at least trying it out. Aubri knew, in her heart, that she couldn't handle people she loved being so far from her for a long time. She made up her mind about it long ago, no matter how much she missed being with Renee. She knew it was her decision, and she was willing to own up to that being the end of their relationship, doomed to never see each other.

And now here she was, at the same resort as her, and likely as a fellow contest winner since she was also on this floor. Aubri couldn't help but wonder if fate was just screwing with her, now. Was this retribution for the decisions she made with her past dating life?

"The internship was pretty fun." Aubri recognized the cute smile Renee always had, the blissful gleam in her eyes whenever she talked about anything she liked. "It was a lot of work, trust me, but it *did* land me a sweet full-time job afterwards. The people overseeing me during the internship liked my work *so* much that they practically offered the position to me a week before the internship ended!"

"Really? Congratulations!" Aubri smiled back at her. She was glad to hear that Renee was doing well in her career life. At least there was something going right in the world, even if it wasn't romance.

"Thanks." Renee smiled back at her, warmer this time, and Aubri couldn't resist her heart fluttering at seeing her smile so radiantly as she did – one of the many reasons she once dated her. "What about you? What have you been up to since graduating university? I saw your grad photos online."

Aubri paused, thinking. Should she tell her about Colin? She decided not to, shrugging. She didn't want her ex-girlfriend being miserable over her messed-up love life. That wasn't something Renee needed to know. "Well…I got a full-time job. Just some office work. Editorial assistant, nothing special."

Renee nodded. "Still good, though."

Aubri shrugged. "True. At least I get to make the magazine spreads looking nice."

Renee nodded again, and Aubri was about to cut the conversation short when Renee spoke up again. "And...what happened between you and Colin?"

Aubri swallowed. She previously hoped Renee dropped most contact with her, post-breakup and wouldn't see anything involving Colin, the boyfriend she had during university. Now that she thought about it, Aubri herself *had* made it more than public enough on her social media to let everyone know that she was no longer dating Colin, especially with all the fighting prior to their breakup. Now she had no choice but to tell Renee. It made sense, Aubri supposed, Renee wanting to know more about this. There were exes, after all.

She willed herself to play it cool as she spoke, but she felt a shiver up her spine despite her best efforts. "You saw that on social media, huh?"

Renee nodded, her smile vanishing. "Yeah. Your ex. Are you okay?"

Aubri's brows furrowed as she nodded. "I'd rather not talk about it, but the short version is: He wasn't great. I'm *glad* I dumped him before I finished my last term of uni." It hadn't been easy, but after she ghosted him post-breakup and avoided every place she'd find him at, he hadn't gone off looking for her. Didn't even try to get back in contact with her, so at least he left her alone. She also didn't want to tell Renee about the situation with Bastian, either. That would make things especially awkward if those two ran into each other by chance, while they were here.

"Well," Renee finally managed, shrugging, "At least we can just have a fun time here. I'll be seeing you around, I guess?"

"Yeah. See you around." Aubri quickly went towards her

room but tried walking at a pace where it didn't seem like she ran away from her ex-girlfriend. She felt her own face flush, and she shook her head, unlocked the door, and stepped inside with her luggage in hand. The last thing she wanted to think about was exes, and yet both were at this resort. Fate must really hate her right now, she supposed.

Aubri's hotel room was certainly spacious. The main entrance area of the hotel room, leading into the living room included a small balcony overlooking the outdoor pool, a dining table with four seats and a smaller kitchen area to cook anything (though Aubri doubted she'd need to cook during this time). There was a master bathroom with lovely-looking, marbled floors attached to the cozy, yet luxurious bedroom with not a queen, but *king*-sized bed in the bedroom. The living room even had a large, flatscreen TV against the wall opposite cozy-looking couches!

Now *this* was a dream hotel room. And it looked even better than the rooms shown online, too. At least this part of her vacation would go right, in Aubri's opinion. In the worst-case scenario if things got too awkward seeing all her ex-fake-boyfriends and ex-girlfriend around, Aubri could just retreat to her room, order room service if she got hungry, and just hole up in here until the rest of the week was over. Right?

She put down her things in the bedroom where she'd sleep for the next seven days and found a note on the bedside table from the staff, congratulating her on winning the contest, and reminding her that room service and additional amenities would be under her own responsibility. The same went for any drinks at the bar unless she got "The Winner's Drink," which was an exclusive specialty drink for all the contest winners. She shrugged, put the note down, before she laid down on the bed and closed her eyes, a sigh leaving her. Getting settled in was awkward enough, with the two random reunions with people she never thought she'd see again. Then again, fate had a funny way of toying with her social life.

CHAPTER 3

After a while of lounging around in her room and unpacking her things, Aubri decided to take a walk around the hotel. It was certainly kept clean as she noticed so far, as there was not a speck of dust anywhere. Heck, there wasn't even any noticeable amount of sand coming into the main building's entrance from the beach. Other hotel guests walked around, enjoying themselves as they chatted with each other or took in the scenery, but at least everyone was nice enough to not make a mess or do anything stupid…for now.

She suspected things might get wild in the evening. Apparently, the bar had a reputation for serving a lot of good drinks, but the trouble of drunk guests came along with it. She smiled as she approached a hot tub only a couple feet away from the main pool area. Maybe she could take a warm soak in there, later. It would be a nice way to unwind from running into Renee and Bastian earlier.

She looked around, just in case there were any odd ex-partners roaming about. She noticed Renee chatting with a few other people she didn't know. Bastian sat across the courtyard with another group of people (though they seemed to be in the middle of a 'matchmaking' event going on, given how there was a hotel staff person clearly leading the group in switching partners at designated times).

Maybe, Aubri realized, it was *just* those two here. Things would be fine if it was just those two. Awkward if she ran into them, but at least she'd be fine.

She looked around one more time, just to check, and then

she saw *him.* The dark hair, brown, leering eyes, and the familiar, arrow-shaped tattoo on his neck that she used to adore. Used to, at least.

She swallowed.

Colin?

Surely, he couldn't be one of the winners. She had to get out of his sight before he spotted her! Her legs carried her as brisk as she could without looking panicked, heading back inside the building and down the hallway, hoping to make it to the lobby, forcing herself to take deep breaths.

Don't think of Colin, she begged herself. Maybe she could walk around the beach for a bit, relax over there and take a few photos. Come back to the actual building when it was closer to dinnertime. If it would help her avoid him, then that was fine. That was perfect. She wanted nothing to do with him, and she'd make sure to everything she could…

"Aubri!"

She ignored the familiar yell and walked even faster. She tried to hope that he would just lose her, that he would just knock it off and leave her alone. She wanted to do nothing but forget about how he tried to pressure her for sex, after he found out about her and Bastian fake-dating each other. How he accused her of being a slut for money despite her insistence that she and Bastian never had sex to begin with.

"Hey! Aubri!"

She walked even faster, but she soon felt a hand on her shoulder. An instinctive scream left her, before she whirled around and punched whoever grabbed her in the face.

"Fuck!" The man (Colin) stepped back, letting go of her as he staggered, trying to keep balance. "What the hell was that for!?"

"Don't just grab me, you *bitch!"* Aubri yelled back, glaring at him. Her hand throbbed, already sore from the punch, but she did her best to ignore it. Colin gazed right back at her, frowning. One of his blue eyes already visibly bruised and starting to swell a bit from the punch. "If I'm walking away from you when you're calling to me, I want to be left alone, okay?"

"Don't tell me *you* fucking won the contest, too." Colin groaned, shaking his head. He didn't take a step closer, but he wasn't on the verge of running off, either. He had a bit more stubble on his face than when she last saw him, but it was still him. "I thought I was having a lucky break from you. Looks like I was wrong."

"That's what I hoped, too. To get away from *you* for once." Aubri swallowed, still staring him down. He won? Why? Why did the universe have to screw with her by bringing along her ex-girlfriend, ex-fake-boyfriend, *and* her ex-boyfriend to this island resort? "If you try to do anything like what you just did again, I *will* report you to the resort staff and get you out of here."

A soft laugh left Colin at that, and Aubri hated that she liked his laugh and smile. There was always a bit of charisma in him, no matter how much she despised him. "That would be a scandal, wouldn't it? Kicking off one of the contest winners from their own resort over the two of us being exes?"

"It's a different story when your ex previously pressured you for sex." Aubri immediately pointed out, raising a brow. "I ghosted you for a good reason, you know. Don't you dare think of getting near me again. Ever." She couldn't stop the icy edge seeping into her voice. She wanted to make it clear that she and Colin weren't getting together, ever, and nothing would change that.

He shrugged, raising his hands lightly in surrender. "Alright, alright, take it easy." He chuckled, and she loved and hated that husky laugh of his. "You stay outta my hair, I stay outta yours. Doesn't seem that hard, does it?"

Try sleeping on the same floor of this hotel and we'll find out, Aubri thought, but a sigh left her. "You better keep your word." He had a history of not doing that.

"Fine."

Aubri turned on her heel and walked straight into the building, hoping that he wouldn't follow her. He didn't, much to her relief.

Despite him not following her, however, a pit formed in her stomach as she let the encounter with him sink in, and she did her best to ignore the dreaded feelings. However, Aubri knew it was an all-too-telling sign that something worse was about to happen. And she didn't know what that could be, but she hoped it wasn't going to happen.

CHAPTER 4

Nighttime fell over the island in a matter of hours, and Aubri, after going out to the sandy beach to just have some time for herself and away from everyone else, did come back to the hotel. After all, she needed dinner. Something good to eat, and maybe a few drinks. Scratch that; *definitely* a few drinks.

There were several fancy restaurants within the resort's main building, but there was also a bar leading out to the pool area where a party-like atmosphere was set up for the evening. Aubri didn't feel right going into a restaurant, given that she'd be eating alone among all the other lovey-dovey couples present there, so she headed straight for the bar. Right away, she already noticed Bastian sitting at the bar, downing the first drink of the night. He looked morose in Aubri's opinion, given his frown and furrowed brows. Hadn't he mentioned something about matchmaking services, earlier? Maybe that didn't end well.

As tempted as Aubri was to join Bastian at the table, she also knew that it was probably not the best idea. There might be questions raised if Renee saw her with him. Or...how would Colin react, if he saw Bastian again? She knew too well that both men did *no*t like each other after all that they went through.

Then again – Bastian was her friend. And Aubri knew that she shouldn't care about what her other exes thought of her. Maybe it wouldn't be a bad idea to see if Bastian at least wanted someone to chat with, so he wasn't so lonely. She took a deep breath, before approaching Bastian's table.

"Hey, Bastian?" She noticed him look up to face her, before she breathed, "Mind if I join you?"

A light grin appeared on Bastian's face, before he nodded. "Please do. I'd like the company."

Both ordered the winners' drink from the menu Bastian had on hand before Aubri spoke up again. "Had any luck with matchmaking? You look kinda down, so I thought…"

"No luck, sadly." He shrugged, shook his head once. Their special drinks were soon served, and Aubri tasted them. They were practically pina coladas; just decorated with gold leaves to make them look fancy. She took a few sips, savouring the sweetness, and then looked up at Bastian as he continued speaking. "Everyone that went to matchmaking was either there for genuine hookups with no whiff of romance whatsoever, or they were old people."

"As old as you?" Aubri teased.

His nose wrinkled at that. "I had to tell *every* single woman that I'm gay. It wasn't fun."

She grimaced, leaning back a little in her seat. "Sorry."

"You don't have to apologize. At least most of them took it well, though a few of them said some pretty homophobic shit that I'd rather not repeat aloud." He finished his glass, just before Aubri saw the bartender look towards them, just as he moved to pick up their now-emptied glasses.

"Homophobes? That's unfortunate. Sorry to hear that, bud." The bartender was cute looking, in Aubri's opinion. Olive skin, golden-brown eyes, and had a bit of dark stubble on the chin, but it was well-trimmed. The man offered Bastian a soft smile – Aubri could tell that the guy couldn't be too much older than her. "How about I get you another Winners' drink, on the house?"

Bastian looked down at the drink, then up at the bartender as a smile appeared on his face. "You just made my night, handsome. Thanks."

The bartender flashed him his own smile. "Whoever passed on you probably wasn't looking closely enough at you, because you look fantastic."

"Really?" Aubri restrained her own chuckle as she watched Bastian continue flirting with the younger man. "And I'm sure whoever you're with is lucky to have you."

The bartender could only sigh, shaking his head. "Sadly, I'm single. Name's Nick."

"Bastian." Bastian smiled, and Nick chuckled lightly at seeing him grin. "Pleasure to meet you."

"Pleasure to meet you too." Nick winked back at him. "Maybe we can chat more, in a bit? My shift finishes in half an hour."

"I'd love that – but get me that drink first, please." Bastian quipped, and Nick offered him one last smile before moving to attend to another customer asking for drinks.

Aubri watched Nick attend to his work, then noticed Bastian's lingering gaze on him. "You like him, don't you?"

Bastian's gaze snapped towards her, staring. "What? He's cute."

"And you're *totally* checking him out." She pointed out, smiling as she noticed Bastian's face flush.

"Not my fault that he's courteous, gets me a free drink, *and* he looks good." Bastian couldn't help but laugh a bit, before shaking his head. "And I'm more than sure he wants more than just chatting after his shift is over."

"Congratulations, then. You just got an invitation for getting laid." Aubri joked, and she saw her companion's face flush slightly.

"I don't think it'd go *that* far, would it? I'm not..." He faltered, before shaking his head. "I mean, I'm kind of old for him. I know that already. He can't be too much older than you."

"Still technically legal." Aubri reminded him, raising a brow. "You're only, what, early forties at this point?" Nick didn't look too much older than Aubri herself, in her opinion, so he had to be in about his mid-to-late twenties.

"Yeah." Bastian hastily took a few more sips, but she could see his flushed face–and it wasn't from the alcohol. "God, *thanks* for making me feel like an old fart."

"Hey! Maybe Nick is into that sort of guy." Aubri elbowed him lightly, offering him a reassuring grin. "I mean, you're the best fake-boyfriend I ever had. Maybe you'll end up being the best *real* boyfriend he's ever had, if things work out between you two."

"Let's take it one step at a time first." He managed, shaking his head. "There's no point if he and I don't click for the first while."

"Oh, I'm sure you both already do." Aubri murmured, smiling back at him. At least there was hope in Bastian's love life. Maybe something could honestly, seriously, go well after all. "Is it okay if I take a celebratory photo of both of us? For being here?"

Bastian hesitated. "You're not going to show my face, are you? You know I'd rather stay private for, well, obvious reasons."

She shook her head, still maintaining a reassuring grin. "I won't even mention your name, promise. I'll keep it vague enough."

He shrugged. "Well, I guess it can't hurt. Go ahead."

She carefully moved their free hands together, intertwining fingers. She positioned her phone so that she could see both hands clearly, but the drinks were at the edges of the screen. She didn't mind. She snapped the photo.

It wasn't hard to think of a vague enough caption, as she typed it out quickly and showed it to him. The caption read, *"Saw a friend today. It's nice to see him here."*

She saw Bastian chuckle at seeing the photo and its caption. "It's nice to see you too, Aubri. Thanks for the privacy."

"No problem."

He paused, then looked towards her, raising a brow. "Trying to make your friends at home jealous?"

"A little," She admitted, before both laughed. The next hour passed with a few more drinks, a bit more food. Thankfully, Aubri knew from experience that both she and Bastian had decent alcohol tolerances, and so they weren't getting drunk too soon.

Amid the warm conversation, however, she heard Renee's familiar voice – and she did not sound pleased, judging by how tense she sounded.

"*What* did you say about her, you jerk!?"

"You heard me, bitch!"

Aubri's gaze snapped towards her left where she heard Colin reply. As far as she could see, Colin and Renee stood opposite each other. Colin looked clearly drunk, what with him staggering about where he stood. "That piece of ass is a sugar baby, didn't you know? Bet she only dated you in high school because you're rich. She just took a good look at all the expensive stuff you carried around with you, I bet, and dug her claws into you!" He snapped. "I *know* that you're the daughter of some big-shot company overseas. That's the only reason you got that internship after high school! Not surprised she dated you."

Aubri noticed Bastian's jaw clench, but he didn't rise from the table, looking towards Aubri. Any relaxed ambiance he had was gone, replaced by a slight shake of his head and a nervous swallow. "Should I leave?" He asked, voice low.

Aubri looked between him, then Colin and Renee. "Yeah. You should."

"We already paid for our other drinks earlier, right?"

"Yup. Why'd you ask?"

He looked her in the eye sheepishly. "Want to escape with me?"

"Sounds great." Aubri quickly finished the last of her drink, hoping to get out of here. The sooner, the better.

She and Bastian quickly got up, both moving to both hide themselves in the surrounding crowd, but they didn't get far before Aubri heard Colin loudly proclaim, "She's a slut for money, Renee! She was sugaring behind my back when we dated!"

Aubri's gut twisted at the statement rang through the bar. Memories of the day Colin found out about her fake-dating Bastian flooded her mind. She wasn't exactly sure how he did it at the time, but looking back at it, she figured that he must have looked at her phone while she wasn't looking. She remembered the ways he started pressuring her for sex, asking her constantly if she'd slept with her "sugar daddy" before, despite her denials about sleeping with Bastian. Eventually, she dumped and ghosted him a few weeks before her last term of uni.

She also ended the fake-dating arrangement with Bastian after *he* found out what went down between her and her ex-boyfriend at the time. Bastian was worried for her safety more than anything, but she'd told him that she'd be fine if she stayed away from her ex.

Earlier, she thought that things would be fine, that Colin would stay out of her way despite being at the same resort at her. Tonight, proved otherwise.

Renee hissed, before punching Colin hard in the face, hard enough for him to stagger back. "You fucking liar! Stop insulting my ex-girlfriend, you asshole!"

Aubri froze. Should she help? Should she get Renee out of there? But at the same time, the word *slut* reached her, and she swallowed, pushing down memories of Colin yelling at her at the back of her mind. She felt a hand on her shoulder, and she looked up towards Bastian, who looked clearly concerned for her, starting to guide her away.

"We should go," He whispered. "Now."

Aubri looked back once, seeing security guards grab both

Renee and Colin to separate them and lug them out of the bar. "But what about…?'

"Our safety comes first." Bastian insisted, shaking his head. "Okay?"

"Need any help?" The two looked towards Nick, who just approached them. Aubri noticed the slight grimace on the man's face as he looked up at Renee and Colin, and then towards Aubri and Bastian. "I can get you both out the back entrance if you want. It's closer to the elevators from there if you're heading upstairs to your rooms."

"Really?" Bastian asked, starting to get up from his seat. "You can do that?"

"Yeah. Follow me!" The bartender nodded, getting out from around the counter before gesturing with a hand for Aubri and Bastian to follow him. "This way."

The three pushed pasted some of the various tables, chairs and so on, nearing the bathrooms. There was a door close to where the bar's bathroom area was, and Aubri figured that must be the back entrance. She watched the Nick take out a key card, sliding it through the door's lock. A beep followed, and the bartender opened the door, letting Aubri and Bastian through.

"Thank you." Bastian managed, just as he and Aubri stepped through.

The bartender nodded, offering both a slight smile. "The elevator's down the hall. I can call your rooms for a follow-up if needed."

"That would be wonderful." Bastian paused, then quipped, "Room 702. That's mine."

"I'm 703." Aubri quickly added.

"702 and 703. Got it." The bartender winked at Bastian. "Have safe night, both of you." With that, he closed the door behind them, letting them both go back to their rooms on their own.

CHAPTER 5

Aubri and Bastian were silent as they stood in the ascending elevator. Aubri wasn't sure if it was just nerves shared between them over what just happened, or if it was because of what words were said by Colin over Aubri.

"That guy was cute. Helpful, too." Aubri managed, leaning back against one wall of the elevator. She hoped to break the silence with something unrelated, something more fun to talk about. Maybe it would salvage this night from everything that happened earlier.

"You mean Nick?" Bastian asked, leaning against the wall opposite her. He had a soft smile on his face, despite all that just happened minutes ago. "I agree. He *is* cute and helpful. And the fact that he helped us escape is helping. Do you think I should get his actual number when he calls my room, later?"

"Maybe you should." Aubri couldn't help but chuckle at that. "He seems nice. And he's probably the sanest man we've met at this resort so far."

"Fair." Both momentarily shared some laughter.

"Didn't think I'd see your ex again." Bastian finally managed, just as a dinging noise resounded through the elevator before the doors opened to reveal their designated floor. His brows furrowed, and he hesitated before asking, "Must suck seeing Colin around, huh? And...who was that other person with him? Friend of yours?"

"Actually," Aubri admitted, looking up at him, "Both of those people fighting were my exes. You know Colin, but the woman, Renee...she was my ex-girlfriend from high school."

A slow groan left Bastian, nose wrinkling at that last statement. "That must be messy."

"It is."

The two stepped into the hallway, and Aubri walked towards her hotel room's door. She paused as she put her hand on the doorknob and then towards Bastian, before asking, "Want to come in? It'll be easier to chat about it." She trusted Bastian – unlike the other exes here in this place, at least they'd parted on the best terms and weren't causing any fights.

Bastian accepted the invitation. He was courteous to take off his shoes and leave them by the door, and Aubri ditched her own heels and changed into cozier slippers she packed with her for this trip. She wordlessly grabbed some snack bags provided to her by the hotel, not caring that she'd probably have to pay for consuming them later, before handing one to him. Both slumped onto the couch, quiet again, before a sigh left Bastian.

"Do you want to talk about it anymore? The exes and..." He gestured with a free hand, "All that?"

She hesitated as she opened her bag of snacks. "Well..."

Aubri knew that Bastian knew too well about what happened between her and Colin, but he didn't know much about Renee. And now that they were on this same level of an odd friendship despite their former connections, maybe it wouldn't hurt to open up a bit. After all, Bastian had only been her fake boyfriend for the sake of getting away from an ex-acquaintance of his own. *Maybe* he'd understand the situation if she told him.

Besides, if they were all going to be stuck here for a week, Aubri realized, it was probably best to tell Bastian the truth of her connections with the other two exes while they were here. Just so he knew exactly how complicated it all was, that is.

"Renee was my ex from high school. We broke up 'because I didn't want a long distance after graduation." Aubri leaned back against the couch, putting her bag of snacks down on her lap. "We were going to try staying in contact at first, but then I couldn't bear with it anymore."

"So...you dumped her?" He concluded, frowning.

"Yeah. She was in the middle of an internship abroad when I did so, too." Aubri grimaced, shaking her head. "I felt bad about doing that, but...it wasn't working. And I didn't want to be half there for her in the relationship we had, considering the distance between us. I dropped all contact with her afterwards, so I'm surprised that we both ended up here, in the same resort of all places."

"Fate has a funny way of bringing people back to us." Bastian munched on a few chips from his bag, before continuing. "Besides, if that wasn't the case, I don't think you would've ended up at this island with me *and* your two other exes."

A faint laugh left at that. "Fair." She smiled. "I suppose you have a point."

"I am glad you told me the truth, though." Bastian's eyes met hers. "And...I appreciate all the clarification."

Aubri offered him a smile back. "I figured you needed an explanation. It wouldn't be fair of me to keep you in the dark. We're friends, right?"

He smiled back at her. "Friends."

Aubri didn't remember when she went to bed and fell asleep, as she and Bastian talked for the rest of the night, but she did. And she'd rest peacefully, despite all that happened earlier. She didn't invite Bastian to her room, obviously, but she let him sleep on the couch. She was thankful it could extend into a spare bed for him, so he didn't have to wander back to his own room so late.

Maybe, she hoped as she slept, things would get better from here.

CHAPTER 6

Aubri woke up, hearing voices echoing from outside. Sitting up in bed, she looked towards the balcony, before checking out what it was. Maybe it was people talking about what happened last night at the bar, or maybe it was something else. Either way, she wanted to know.

As she got out of bed, she peeked outside her bedroom, only to realize that Bastian wasn't on the couch. The couch itself was even set back to normal, despite her unfolding it for him last night. He must have let himself out, she figured. She noticed the phone on the desk blinking, a sign of a message, and she decided to check it first.

"Good early morning, room 703. Miss Aubri Celestia Harlow, right?" She recognized the bartender's voice. Nick was his name, right? *"I hope you and 702 slept well after all that happened last night. To help make up for the horrid experience in the bar last night, we're offering both of you all the free drinks on the house for the remainder of your stay."* There was a pause, then a sigh. *"Honestly, though, I would be happy if I got 702's number. And I don't mean by his hotel room number, since I already have that. Anyway, I hope you have a swell time for the remainder of your stay!"*

The machine beeped afterwards, and Aubri heard someone scream from outside. She dashed back into her bedroom, towards the balcony, and…

That was when Aubri saw Colin. He lay on the ground by the pool, motionless. Blood pooled around his whole figure, some of the blood dripping into the pool and staining the water a light red, and she couldn't make out his face from the whole thing from the far distance between her and him. The person who screamed at the dead Colin swooned, and a couple of bystanders caught her in their arms.

Is he…dead?

Only last night, Aubri remembered seeing him alive and angry, given his fight with Renee. But now here he was, motionless, and deceased.

Was it a murder?

She didn't know *why* she immediately thought it could be a murder. But what else could it be, if not an accident?

"Step aside, please." Aubri heard one of the hotel staff speak up, and Aubri saw the guests move aside in time for some of the staff, plus security, to approach Colin. Several of the staff began covering up the corpse in some tarp. She heard a knock on the main door, and she rushed out of her bedroom and towards the main door of her suite to answer it.

She opened the door to find a note on the floor, and Aubri picked it up to read the following:

"To our beloved guests of the Calloway Resort,

One of our guests has been found dead, at the pool earlier this morning at 6 a.m. Due to the cleanup, as well as further investigations, the pool area will be closed for the remainder of today, and will reopen tomorrow morning at 10 a.m.

As much as we wish that the police will reach the island soon, we regret to inform all of you that they will not arrive until exactly one week from today, due to inclement weather predicted for at least the next three to four days.

To secure the safety of our guests so this type of incident does not happen again, we will be installing further security measures including the following:

> 1. *There will be an increase in security patrolling the island, especially in the nighttime from 7 p.m. to 7 a.m.*

2. *Certain facilities will be closing earlier until further notice to ensure the safety of both guests and staff.*
3. *Guests are encouraged to attend any of the resort's facilities in groups of two-to-three people, minimum.*
4. *All guests must be in their rooms by 10 p.m. and cannot leave until 7 a.m. Anyone caught between those hours will be questioned immediately.*

Below is the new list of our facilities' open hours. All of these are effective immediately until further notice..."

Aubri put the note down, closing the door. She walked over to the nearby dining table, a sigh leaving her as she sat down in a chair beside it.

What now? There was a murderer on the loose, and Aubri knew too well that said murderer killed Colin, her ex-boyfriend. What if the murderer was after her and the others who won this contest? Were they jealous that they got to come here for free? Aubri was more than aware that there *were* probably people jealous of the winners. She vaguely recalled a few guests eyeing her winners' drink from last night, while she was talking with Bastian. Maybe they thought Colin was easy bait and killed him, in the dead of night? But *how?* And *when,* exactly, last night?

There was another knock on the door, and Aubri swung it open to see none other than Bastian, who held up a copy of the note she received. "You saw the news?"

Aubri held up hers, nodding once. "Just did. *Please* don't tell me you killed him while I was asleep."

"Aubri, I understand that you love murder mysteries, and this seems entirely suspicious, but I was literally with you last night. How could I have murdered him?" Bastian raised a brow. "I only woke up and walked back to my room half an hour ago to get changed, and then I found the note just now."

Aubri frowned. Half an hour ago, she was still asleep. It made sense that Bastian let himself out to get back to his own room, given how she saw the couch be folded back into its normal position compared to last night. And if he was here the whole night up until then, and the corpse wasn't discovered until before he left this room, then he *couldn't* have murdered Colin. She took a deep breath, relaxing her shoulders, before opening the door a bit wider. "Come in."

He immediately walked in, and she shut the door behind her, staring up at him. "I can't believe this happened." She managed, shaking her head. The last thing she *wanted,* during a vacation, was someone getting murdered, even if she was a big fan of all the fictional murder mysteries. No one should be getting murdered while on vacation, of all times! That was just *wrong!*

He swallowed, grimacing. "My question is, where are they going to store the body until the police comes? The hotel's restaurant meat freezer?"

She shuddered, trying not to imagine it. That was often a detail that most mystery novels she read tended to gloss over. "I don't think I want to know."

"Sorry."

The two decided that they should continue this conversation over breakfast, and promptly called for room service. After the food arrived, they ate at the dining table in awkward silence. Trying to have a casual conversation with each other over breakfast, after seeing that someone just died, seemed like bad timing. As she finished her meal, Aubri couldn't help but ask, "Do you think the killer will come after us next?"

Bastian shrugged. She noticed his shoulders were slightly raised, but he tried not to show any tenseness on his face. "Well, he, she or they killed your ex. I wouldn't be surprised if they tried going after us next. And the police aren't coming until a week from now, so...that gives them a lot of time to finish the job, doesn't it?"

"Ohmygod." Aubri sank into her seat as she finished her

toast. "Of *all* the times I go on a vacation, I got stuck with my exes and former classmate *and* someone was murdered."

"To be fair," Bastian shrugged as he finished eating his toast, "you only must deal with only one ex, now. The other one is dead."

She wasn't sure if she shouldn't be laughing at hearing his remark, but she did it anyway. "Still, though. Doesn't make it any less shitty for us."

He nodded. "Fair. What do we do, then? Hide in our rooms for seven days straight?" She raised a brow at his statement, and he could only sigh as he looked her in the eye, frowning. "What? It makes sense. It's the logical thing to do, right?"

"That *would* be the easy way out, but probably the safest..." Aubri paused, taking a deep breath. What if the killer did really go after the rest of them? Her, Renee and Bastian?

And if the police weren't coming to this island to find the killer for them, well...who else was going to do it for them other than herself? Sure, there was the hotel staff, but they would likely be more occupied with ensuring the other guests' safety rather than looking for a murderer. Maybe, Aubri thought, could do it. She was a big fan of all the detective mystery books, shows, and so on. Mysteries were always something she loved exploring. So, why not explore this one- especially since it might concern her and the other remaining winners, in the first place? They had enough experience reading and watching mysteries to know what to do right, right?

Aubri looked Bastian in the eye. "I have an idea."

He stared at her, before shaking his head. "If you're thinking of trying to play detective, then no. I'm not helping with this."

"What?" She stared at him. "But you *love* murder mystery books! This is your thing! We literally bonded over this in class, back in uni!" Hell, back when they even fake-dated, they binge-watched a ton of mystery shows together! Why would he back out now when there was a real mystery right here and now?

He shook his head again. "It does *not* work like how it does in all the mystery books and shows, Aubri! It's called *fiction* for a reason. Otherwise, that's true crime *nonfiction*, not murder mystery fiction."

"The police aren't going to be here for a week, Bastian." Aubri insisted, raising a brow at him. "If we can find at least a *lead* on who potentially killed Colin, we can tell the police what we found by the time they arrive. Even if we can't find out who *exactly* the killer is, we can at least help the police that way. The longer you let something go uninvestigated, the better the killer hides their tracks. That's a basic plan in *all* the murder mysteries we've read and watched!"

He frowned. "You have a fair point, but…what if the killer finds out we're trying to investigate them and tries to kill us?"

"The killer might possibly try to kill us next regardless of whether we investigate or not. All four of us on this floor are winners of the contest, and one of us is already dead after day one." Aubri shrugged, and tried not to shudder too much as she let that sink in. One of them was dead. Would there be more dead bodies on the way, if they didn't start investigating? "What are we supposed to do until the police arrive? Hide in our rooms for the remainder of our vacation?"

Bastian gave her a look. "That was literally the plan I just proposed earlier."

"That's true, but I'd *really* rather not hide, if I don't have to. If we can do something about this, this can all be resolved faster." She paused, then raised a brow. "So? Are you in?"

He paused, then sighed, shaking his head before looking her in the eye. "Only to try to prevent *you* from getting killed. And myself, of course. So *yes,* I will help you."

"Good. Because we're starting now!" She beamed right back

at him, before she grabbed the free notepad provided on the desk, before ripping off a few pages after grabbing a pen from said desk, starting to write down a list. Despite the harrowing danger, she felt a strange lightness in her chest, a smile still on her face. "We need to form a plan for this whole investigation. We should ask all the hotel staff we can, discreetly, about finding Colin dead. We should also ask about who last saw him before he died. They could be suspects."

Bastian simply chuckled as Aubri began writing a to-do list, and she noticed him smile wryly. "If any of those bring me opportunities to see Nick, I'd like to be involved in them. And by the way, I *did* leave him my number after he called me earlier about having free drinks for the rest of our stay here."

"Nice." Aubri noted, giving him a brief high-five before she continued speaking. "I did remember him saying he wanted your number after he left a message to me about it. He must've called me before he called you, at the time." She paused in her writing, scanning her to-do list as follows:

To-do:

- *Ask hotel staff about Colin*
- *Ask others that saw him before he died?*
- *Don't get killed.*

"What about Renee?" Bastian pointed out.

Aubri looked up from her list, frowning. "Renee? Why are we bringing her up?"

He raised a brow. "She and Colin were duking it out prior to his death. She literally punched him in the face last night at the bar. Doesn't that make her a suspect, in some capacity?"

Aubri shook her head. "I don't know if one punch in the face qualifies her as a potential killer, Bastian."

He raised a brow. "It's a possible clue, though. And sure, maybe it's an occasional red herring in all the mystery novels we've read, but it's still worth looking into. Jealous exes are a common trend in murder mysteries, after all. Same with exes fighting each other over the same person!"

Aubri sighed "Okay, that's a good point. But we also need to be careful. So, we can't fuck with curfew too much or else we might get locked in our rooms for the whole rest of the time, and then we can't do a thing. We should try to adhere to the curfew for now."

With that in mind, she wrote the following:

- *Stick with curfew (BE BACK IN ROOM BY 10 P.M.) unless given good reason to break it.*
- *Do NOT be alone if you don't have to. (Unless it's something like going to the washroom. That makes more sense.)*

"What if we got to the point of breaking into people's rooms to find information?" Bastian asked. "Do you think we could try that?"

Aubri stared at him. "That is a bad idea in *so* many ways."

"Still." He supplied, "We might have to do that. If the killer is on this island, in this building, it's likely that they might be a guest or a staff person sleeping here."

She grimaced. She wasn't sure if she wanted to start with that, for many reasons. How would she break into people's rooms these days, anyway? Steal their key cards to get in? "Let's try not to worry about this yet if the situation doesn't call for it. As far as we know right now, there are too many people we could suspect as the killer. I think we need to find out how Colin died and get that evidence first."

She saw him smile. "Where do we start with that, then?"

Aubri smiled back at him. "How about we ask the staff, first? Maybe they saw someone follow him to his room after the fight at the bar last night." She would have suggested checking out the pool area where Colin landed, or Colin's own room, but both places were unfortunately off bounds and the pool area was already cleaned by the hotel staff at this point. (Aubri wished, deep in her heart, that she learned how to pick locks. It would've been convenient for investigating Colin's room.)

"Good place to start." He gave her a nod, and Aubri did her best to restrain her own excitement at taking on this investigation. "Let's do it."

Aubri and Bastian both made it downstairs after they both finished breakfast and got changed for the day, before taking the elevator down. A tingle shuddered through Aubri's spine as they descended to the main floor. She didn't really know if it was a good idea, investigating the murder themselves, but she also knew that she didn't want to get killed. And if she could find out who killed Colin before the killer got to her, Bastian, or Renee sooner, the better things might be soon. As they were stepping out of the elevator, however, she heard Renee shouting.

"I demand a further explanation!"

"I'm sorry," An older woman's voice spoke up, "but I can't tell more at this time."

Aubri turned to see none other than Renee speaking (or, rather, *arguing)* with an older woman, who looked about in her late thirties to early forties. The older woman, olive-skinned with dark brown eyes and black horn-rimmed spectacles, had her brown hair in a bun, wearing a black pencil skirt with the magenta blouse. Renee looked distraught, despite the sunny floral dress and the perfectly matching purse she held today. "Is that…?"

"The hotel manager." Bastian managed, brows furrowing. "Nessandra Thomson. I read up on her and the rest of the hotel's upper management before I came here."

"What will be done about any of this?" Renee asked, swallowing. She looked like she might cry, given the mostly visible tears at the corners of her eyes. Aubri couldn't stop her worries for

Renee from getting to her, just seeing her in such a state. "Why can't I just leave the island? *Obviously,* I'm in danger. This can't be right!"

"This has never happened before. If we let anyone leave the island now, there's a possibility that the murderer will escape. We can't allow that." Nessandra managed, shaking her head. "We must protect the guests until police arrive and secure the area, and until they arrive, we'll be tightening security measures. We mentioned that in the letter we sent to your room, as well as all the other guests' rooms. All the staff are trained in self-defence and security, but I'll have to rearrange some of the extracurricular activities to take place earlier in the day, or just finish early. Until then, I encourage you to stay safe and follow the measures we have in place right now."

"I'm calling my mom about this. She's going to be *pissed* to find out I'm stuck on the same island as the murderer! And *maybe* I should just let everyone know on social media about your horrible strategies and ruin this place! No one should even be getting murdered here in the first place!"

Nessandra frowned, still refusing to budge despite how Renee cried and complained. Aubri betted that the older woman had too much experience handling difficult clients. And as much as she sympathized for Renee, she also felt equally as bad for the manager at this point. Surely a murder couldn't be good for business. "I'm sure your mother would likely agree with keeping you and the other guests safe from the murderer, with these precautions in place, as well as keeping that murderer from escaping justice. If you are seriously concerned about your safety, however, I'd recommend not being alone whenever you're outside your suite."

"So, you're saying I should just hide in there for the remainder of *my* well-won vacation? Fat chance, bitch!" Renee stormed off, towards the back door leading out towards the resort's built-in greenhouse/garden area. Aubri paused, before running after her. It wasn't right for Renee to be upset like this. Aubri knew that. She wanted to comfort her, let her know that things would be okay. Even if they were exes, that didn't mean that Aubri couldn't *care* about Renee.

"Aubri!" Aubri heard Bastian call, but Aubri ignored him. Renee was upset. And sure, Renee was her ex-girlfriend, but it was clear she was distressed. After all, Renee was just stuck in the same situation as her, Bastian, and the other guests; just in danger like them. Aubri knew that if there was anything anyone needed in this situation, it was comfort. And just because they were broken up didn't mean that Aubri couldn't offer comfort of some sort.

It didn't take long to find Renee despite how fast she ran, wandering one of the various hallways leading to the spa area of the hotel. Renee hadn't gone into the spa. She forced a sigh out of herself and sat on a bench outside the entrance, before burying her head in her hands. Aubri approached her quickly, taking a deep breath. "Renee? Are you okay?"

Renee took a deep breath, looking up at Aubri. It was clear she was crying, given her reddened eyes, and tears threatened to continue spilling out despite doing so earlier.

"I don't want to die," Renee half-spat, shaking her head. She wrapped her arms around herself still as she kept speaking. "Aubri, I just want to go home."

Aubri sat down on the bench beside her, and she was tempted to hug her. She used to do that, back when they were dating. Whenever Renee was upset, all she really needed was a good, long hug. She knew it wouldn't fix everything, but at least it might make her feel better.

However, that was when they were dating, not now. As ex-girlfriends, this was different now. Aubri knew she couldn't give her a hug, because it would just bring up feelings from the past that she didn't need now.

"I'm sure they'll catch whoever the murderer was." Aubri

finally managed, slowly inhaling. "I don't understand why someone would do that, though."

"I-I don't know. Probably jealous." A rough laugh escaped Renee, and she looked towards Aubri, straight into her eyes as her brows furrowed. "You don't...think I did it, do you?"

"What? *No!*" Aubri shook her head. "That's a stupid thing." At least, she hoped, Renee didn't murder anyone. Even then, though, she couldn't help but recall the fight she witnessed last night. Could Renee feel protective over Aubri to the point of killing Colin herself?

Renee's nose wrinkled, before she sighed, shaking her head. "Colin was telling me, last night...before he died, that you were... with some other guy? That you were someone's sugar daddy? Is that true?"

Aubri knew she couldn't hide the truth from her. She wished she could, but it wouldn't help either of them right now. "Yes and no. I wasn't a sugar baby, Renee. He's a close friend of mine from uni, and he asked if I could pretend to be his girlfriend to chase off a former acquaintance trying to get into his pants, despite him telling them that he was gay and uninterested in her. I also really needed the money to pay back my student loans." She tried not to look Renee in the eye. She wasn't sure how her ex-girlfriend would take it.

"So..." Renee swallowed. "Did you and him...?"

"We didn't fuck, Renee. As I mentioned earlier, he's gay. He's not interested in women that way – let alone me." Aubri half-spat out the words, frowning. "The most I did was just hug and pose for a few photos with my face obscured while we were out for dinner or something, but nothing super-suggestive. After Colin found out *and* after I broke up with him, I dropped all contact with Bastian for each other's safety." Aubri decided that she didn't want to go into full details about how Colin and she broke up. Not now. All the details she just told Renee were already a lot.

Renee frowned, nodding slightly. "And now, by coincidence, your ex-fake-boyfriend is here?"

"Yep. He won the contest like the both of us and Colin did." A groan left Aubri's lips as she shook her head. "This is something out of my worst nightmare, I swear."

Renee frowned. "What do you mean? You expected someone to die?"

"No. Just the fact that you, Colin, and Bastian *all* had to be here at once…let alone, *also* winners of this stupid contest." Aubri balled both hands into fists temporarily, shaking her head as she broke eye contact with Renee. "I wish I hadn't entered, now. I wouldn't be stuck in this situation if I was."

"But if you hadn't, I wouldn't have found you again." Renee took a deep breath, looking Aubri in the eyes. "I know this is sudden, but…don't you ever…miss us?"

"Us?" Aubri repeated, looking up to meet her gaze. *Please no. Is she implying…?*

"When we were dating." Renee swallowed. She averted her gaze from Aubri briefly, but when she looked up at her again, Aubri saw tears forming in the corners of her eyes. "I hated breaking up with you. I know you meant well, for both of us, but I want to be back with *you.*"

I knew it. Aubri closed her eyes, trying to process that. Of course, Renee had to miss both dating each other like they used to. *Why now? Why this?* Aubri made up her mind that she would move on, after Renee. She wasn't about to backtrack now. Even if she still cared for her, things were much different now.

"Renee," Aubri sighed, "it's been *years* since we broke up. I've tried moving on already." Why else would she briefly date Colin, after all?

"Obviously," Renee quipped, raising a brow, "it didn't end well."

"No. It didn't." She admitted, before shaking her head. "And given everything right now, I don't know if we should get back together."

"We can always try." Renee whispered, and it was only then at that moment that Aubri realized Renee leaned in towards her. Close enough to *kiss,* even. It was tempting to lean in and kiss her, tell her that she still loved her, but Aubri knew better. This wasn't what she wanted. Instead, she pulled her own head away from Renee, shaking her head.

"Renee, no."

Renee faltered, staring up at Aubri. "What?'

"We can't do this. *I* can't do this. You deserve someone better. Someone that could be better with long-distance relationships, and all of that. I'm not the right person for you, and it's best that you move forward." Aubri stood up, taking a step back. She needed to get away from Renee and this topic entirely – or else it would be too painful for her to bear again.

Renee shook her head, standing and taking Aubri's hands in hers. "Aubri, I'm not going anywhere for a while after I come back home from this vacation, whenever that is. We can start anew. We can try again." She swallowed, squeezing Aubri's hands in her own. "I *know* you didn't want to leave me in the first place. It's not like we dropped our relationship on bad terms."

Aubri just let go of Renee's hands, let them drop to her sides. "I don't think I can. I don't want to take that chance, okay?" Aubri stood, shaking her head. Even as Renee looked at her with a still-sad gaze, Aubri knew she didn't want to open a new can of worms. "I'm sorry. I can't."

Renee bit the inside of her lower lip, and her lashes looked strewn with held-back tears, ready to drip. Instead, she turned her head away from Aubri, and took a deep breath. "Well. If that's what *you* want, then."

Aubri looked away from Renee and left her, not looking

back. She knew she couldn't focus on the possibility of her and Renee getting back together. Not now. Right now, she had a murder to solve, and her own safety to worry about.

CHAPTER 7

Aubri knew that she had to ask the hotel staff about how they found Colin's corpse and try to glean what information she could.

Though the pool was closed, the bar was still open. There were only a few people there, in contrast to the larger crowd from last night. The bar technically wasn't open yet, as it wasn't even close to lunch hours opening. However, there were some staff members present, cleaning up and speaking with each other. Aubri immediately recognized one of them; it was the bartender from last night, the one who flirted with Bastian and helped both him and Aubri escape through the bar's back door when Colin and Renee had their fistfight. His name was Nick, right? The other person with him was blonde, with a plain face and wearing a similar staff uniform.

"Can't believe that guy got killed." Nick sighed, shaking his head as he polished a few glasses. "Lisa, you saw 'him earlier this morning, right?"

The woman working with him shuddered as she wiped the tables. "Can't believe we had to stuff him in the walk-in fridge, too. *That's* what I hate most about it."

He groaned, shaking his head as he wiped the counter. "The owner's going to be *pissed* when she finds out one of the contest winners died. Poor guy."

Aubri herself didn't really pity Colin all that much, given that he was her ex-boyfriend, but she also agreed that it didn't mean he deserved murder. "Excuse me?" She spoke up, approaching them. "Good morning. I was wondering if I could ask about earlier…"

Nick looked up at her sheepishly, offering her a faint grin that looked like a grimace. "Oh, sorry, but the bar is still closed for another two hours. I'm afraid we don't serve drinks in until it's brunch."

"It's fine." Aubri managed, shrugging. "I don't need a drink. I was just wondering…um, the guy that was killed this morning…" She swallowed, "He was sleeping in the room beside mine. I was wondering if I could learn a little more about how you found him. If you don't mind, that is?"

She gave them the best doe-eyes possible, hoping that they might bend to her curious pleas. The woman named Lisa sighed, before looking towards her.

"Well…I *suppose* if you want to know," She shrugged a little, frowning softly. "I saw him at about six in the morning, already dead. He was bleeding into the pool from his head." A shudder left her, before she continued. "Given what me and the other staff saw last night with his drunken fight at the bar, and that he looked like he died from a pretty harsh impact, well…he probably got drunk and fell off the balcony from his room last night. That's what me and the others mostly guess. We're not sure."

Aubri frowned. She remembered Colin being drunk and fighting with Renee last night, just before she and Bastian fled, for sure. How could Colin be drunk *and* get all the way to his room by himself with no problem, only to stumble off his own balcony?

"Did he get escorted back to his room?" She asked. "I can't imagine he went up the elevator by himself, with him being so inebriated."

Lisa shook her head. "Nah, he went off by himself. Stumbled into an open elevator the last time anyone saw him, as far as the rest of us observed. I'm guessing he wasn't entirely drunk if he could do that."

That explained how he got back to his room, for sure. But

that *didn't* explain how Colin fell off the balcony. Unless he was recklessly drunk enough…but something just didn't add up.

"The only other alternative is murder. That's what I heard a couple security guards whispering about, when they lugged his dead body into the freezer." Nick muttered, shaking his head. He then frowned, before looking up at Aubri. "Did you and your friend see him last night, after I escorted you out from the bar?"

"Not since we saw him fighting with Renee last night." Aubri gestured to the rest of the bar, frowning. "We went straight to our rooms after you escorted us out of the bar and stayed there until morning." It wasn't a complete lie – sure, Bastian stayed over in Aubri's room for most of the night until the wee early hour of the morning, but they hadn't left the room during the night at least.

"Who's Renee?" Nick tilted his head, brows furrowing. "The fourth winner." Aubri quickly answered. "The one who fought with Colin, by the way."

"Oh, *her.*" Lisa' lips twisted uncomfortably. "Yeah, security separated those two shortly after they started fighting, and Colin got escorted out of the bar. He stomped off to the elevator after that."

"And that's the last you saw of him?" Aubri asked. "What about Renee?"

"The lady he fought with?" Lisa shrugged, pushing a few bangs out of her face. "She stormed into the pool area briefly, but then she went to the elevators, too. She probably went back to her room to sulk, but that's all I can guess. Not like I can read minds or anything."

Nick nodded. "Yeah. Sorry, that we can't help any further." He paused, before leaning in and asking, "What about your friend, 702? Bastian's his name, right? Is he okay?"

"He's okay. And yes, his name is Bastian." Aubri quickly reassured him, before she recalled Nick's voicemail. She might as well do some digging about him and Bastian while she was talking to him, right? See if those two could hit it off with each other. It was the least she could do as a friend, even if she was in the middle of a murder investigation! "I heard your voicemail from last night."

A soft "Oooh" came from Lisa at that, and she smiled thinly, raising a brow towards her co-worker. "Trying to net a hookup on the job, Nick? Nice try."

Nick's face flushed a little as he looked towards Lisa. "Hey, he's handsome. And he seems like a good guy." His gaze snapped towards Aubri, blinking. "*Is* he a good guy?"

Aubri nodded quickly. "Oh yeah." She managed. "He is. I've known him since uni. We were classmates. I can confirm that he's a *great* guy." After all, he had been her fake-boyfriend for a brief while. And even if the dates were, well, fake, Bastian *had* been a courteous date. Pulled the chair out for her to sit in at restaurants, patiently waited for her outside the bathroom if she got drunk and needed someone to take her back to her dorm building,

"Cool." A chuckle escaped Nick, before he looked Aubri in the eye again. "If you run into Bastian, let him know that I'd be happy to serve him more drinks. I've got another shift later today if he's interested in seeing me."

Aubri chuckled. "I'll let him know. Thanks." She bid the staff farewell and went on her way, before she looked up at the building, towards the top floor.

She immediately noticed that the balcony doors of Colin's room were open. Why was that? Was it open from last night when he died?

Would going into his room, perhaps, give Aubri a better, more concrete idea as of how he died?

Aubri had an idea. A horrible, awful idea. She knew it was one of the things that she and Bastian agreed to not do, but desperate times called for desperate measures. It might be the only way to get evidence, so she figured she might as well bounce this off her budding detective. Why not try it out?

CHAPTER 8

"Bastian, I have to break into Colin's room."

"What?" Bastian stared at her. Aubri texted him earlier, asking him to meet back in her room, and the moment she opened the door to face him, she couldn't help but blurt out the idea. His frown, however, showed obvious disagreement. "You're kidding me, right?"

"No." Aubri shook her head, letting Bastian into the room, closing the door behind her before she continued explaining. "Colin went up to his room before he died last night. The other staff said that he left the bar after security kicked him out, after his and Renee's fight, and then he was last seen into the elevator, presumably up to his own room. And I know, from previously dating him, that he wants to be alone when he's pissed off, no matter how drunk he is. It would make sense if he went straight up to his suite after the fight."

He raised a brow at her statement, tilting his head lightly. "Even when he's obviously drunk?"

Aubri nodded. "Mhm. *Especially* when he's drunk. Someone must have used the opportunity to kill him just as he was entering his room. They probably pushed him off the balcony while he was incoherent."

"You have a point." He paused, before asking, "Does the staff know if he died from the fall or got killed *before* he fell?"

Aubri frowned. "Why ask *that?*"

"The last episode of a show I watched had someone die from getting a head wound and then the murderer covered it up by pushing them off the balcony and splitting their head open *even more*. If Colin suffered a major head wound and *that* led to his death, someone could have hit him in the head when initially attempting to kill him, and then dropped him off the balcony while he was stunned or almost dead enough, to hide the actual cause. They always do this to frame it like a huge accident!"

She shuddered. Even though she could imagine all the scenes Bastian described in full detail, it was still a disturbing image. "You make it sound like *you* killed him." She managed, a soft laugh leaving her – more mortified than she hoped for, despite trying to lighten the mood. "Are you sure you didn't kill him?"

A heavy sigh left him, but she noticed him smiling lightly. "As fun as a plot twist that would be, Aubri, I didn't. I was literally in your room the whole night, remember?"

"Right. Sorry." Aubri paused, then remembered what Nick told her earlier. "By the way, Nick was there when I was asking the staff. He said that he's making drinks tonight if you want to get any from him."

"Really? I might just take him up on that offer." A brief chuckle left him as he shook his head. "I get what you mean, but it's more than obvious that I'm not the killer. And I doubt you're the one that murdered him either, so…who *does* that leave?"

"Do you *still* think it's Renee?" Aubri swallowed. Bastian seemed awfully intent on pinning Renee as the main culprit, in her opinion, though she didn't want to say that aloud just yet.

He nodded. "She's the only one that has a room up here other than you, me, and Colin. Isn't that reasonable, to assume that anyone who has access up here would make the effort to murder him? And if it's not you or me, and Colin's dead unless he offed himself by accident, then Renee is a possible suspect."

Aubri shook her head. Renee was a lot of things to her; her first girlfriend, her first serious relationship before the breakup, and someone she wished she didn't have to break up with. But a killer? That didn't seem right to her. "She seemed pretty upset about his death, Bastian, even if she got into a fight with him the night before. I don't think anyone who would murder him in cold blood would outright be *sad* about it afterwards."

"It could be an act. The widow disposing of her deadbeat husband kind of thing, except they're not married in this case." If Bastian had a board full of notes and ropes attached to each other right now, Aubri could see him being the walking, talking version of a conspiracy theory-related meme. "Again, we see this in half of the crime shows on TV these days." A groan left him at that as he leaned against the wall. "Really, we *need* some more inventive cases that don't involve people getting dismembered or something gruesome like that."

"That's just weird to ponder right now, considering everything that we know about Renee, Colin, and ourselves." Aubri sighed, brows furrowing.

He shrugged. "It could work, though. What if they were previously married? What if they're also *each other's* exes?"

She glared at him. "Much like you, Bastian, Renee is also *gay*, unlike me, who is as bisexual as I can be. There's *no* way she would have willingly married him."

He threw up his hands a little, shaking his head. "Maybe she…might've found out *otherwise*, during the time you two were broken up? We can't just assume completely. We both know that too well!"

Aubri knew she couldn't argue with *that.* "Okay, that's a fair speculation. However, I'm pretty sure she still wants *me*." She stressed. "She literally asked me if we could get back together when I confronted her earlier."

He shrugged. "Well, your ex-boyfriend is dead, so…I'm not surprised if you two actually *do* want to get together, now that he's literally out of the way and not bothering you anymore."

"Yeah. Fair. But…" Aubri shook her head. "I have more

things to worry about right now, like my own safety. And I don't think I'm the right person for her in the end, either." After all, Aubri knew that she was the one that ended things back then, not Renee. "I loved her, Bastian, but I don't think I'm ready for any new romances or rekindling old ones. Especially not now."

"Good point. Staying alive *should* be a priority." Bastian paused, then took a deep breath as he frowned. "What now, then? We just go sneak into Colin's room by getting onto his open balcony, like you suggested earlier?"

Aubri nodded quickly in agreement. "I think climbing onto his balcony is the best situation. His balcony door is still open even after he died. I don't think any of the staff went into his room yet, since they want to preserve the crime scene for when the police come. Is your suite right beside his, by any chance?"

Bastian nodded. "Yes."

She snapped her fingers, smiling. "Perfect. Then I can get there from your balcony. We just need rope, or something we can use to throw across to his balcony to the other side."

"Are you sure about this? Do you have the strength to climb onto someone's balcony from my room?" Bastian called, as Aubri moved to grab the curtains from the window. "But we need an anchor of some sort. A chair, maybe?"

"Never told you before now, but I *did* go to circus camp when I was a kid. I wanted to be a contortionist that was also a detective in one of the books I read, so I begged my mom to sign me up!" Aubri called back as she tugged at the curtains. "I don't know. Let's look for what we can find that won't break easily. Also, can you help me get these off so we can make some rope?"

A relenting sigh left him, and she couldn't help but laugh at that. If this wasn't a murder they were investigating for real, this would be a hilarious situation, trying to sneak on someone's balcony.

Eventually, the two decided on a chair as a makeshift 'anchor' so the end of the rope would stay on Colin's balcony without it falling off and hanging down for others to see. As for the 'rope' to use to get to one balcony to another, Bastian and Aubri decided to use two things:

1. The curtains that were in their rooms. They tied them together as best as they could, and then attached a chair to one end.
2. They tried to use some emergency rope they found in the closets of their suites to also tie the curtains together further so nothing would get torn or fall apart mid-climbing. Probably not the best idea, but it was worth a shot.

Being the lighter of the two, Aubri decided she would be the one climbing to the other balcony. Bastian, meanwhile, would keep watch to make sure the rope didn't break.

The good news was that the distance between both balconies was rather short; in fact, they were only three metres apart from each other due to the wide width of said balconies. It would be easy enough to reach if they threw one end of the rope to Colin's balcony and it ended up latching itself to the railing, due to the heavy-enough weight of the chair attached to said rope's end. The bad news was that there were no proper footholds that one could make out of the walls of the hotel building, so if Aubri fell, she would die.

After throwing the chair to the other balcony and tugging on the rope to test to see if it fell apart or not, Aubri decided to climb across. Wrapping her ankles around the rope and grabbing onto said rope with her hands, she let her bodyweight hang from the makeshift rope carefully as she inched her way across as fast as she could. Thankfully, the knots she and Bastian made were working well enough to support her weight, and she made it across with little difficulty.

All she hoped was that no one spotted her climbing across the balcony.

Colin's balcony door was open, and Aubri carefully stepped into his suite. It was identical to hers in terms of general furniture, curtains, etc. but she could tell something was off.

Shattered glasses on the floor, wine bottle included. Pillows strewn about. The sign of a struggle was present. She tried to picture what a drunk Colin might've tried, in his defense, trying to picture what he did to her when they fought each other, in their past relationship.

He was usually physical in their aggressive interactions, back when they dated. When they fought, he'd grab her by the wrist, or shoulder. Usually she punched him afterwards, and then he'd try to grab her again. After enough resistance, however, he'd usually stomp away or run off somewhere, before coming back hours later to apologize and ask her to take him back.

Of course, this was different. This was an attempted murder that *succeeded.* Whoever fought him probably didn't let him run off. And given that the balcony doors were wide open...

She took pictures of the broken furniture strewn about, as well as the open balcony doors. *The staff mentioned that he likely died from falling off the balcony.* She betted that the killer just finished him off for good, just as Bastian speculated earlier. If Colin was injured in any way prior to dying, like getting bashed in the head, the impact made from him falling off the balcony would easily cover it up.

She checked Colin's bedroom, bathroom, and the kitchenette area for any other signs that might be suspicious, but there wasn't anything odd. They were, in fact, undisturbed. Aubri figured it meant all the fighting took place in the main sitting area and balcony.

She was about to leave the room, head back to the balcony and go across that rope to make it back to Bastian's room, when something familiar on the floor caught the corner of her eye: A black scarf, embroidered with pink flowers. Aubri recognized it was a gift she got Renee once, for her birthday. It was the last gift she ever got for her, too, before they broke up. For a moment, she wished she still dated Renee.

She shook her head. *Focus, Aubri. You have a case to solve… and…why is it in Colin's room, then, of all places? Unless…*

She took a deep breath, looking between the balcony and the scarf on the ground. Should she take it? It could be evidence, she reasoned. She did take a few spare plastic zip-lock bags for this purpose, after all. Seeing it only added to what Bastian told her about suspecting Renee, and she shuddered. Surely, he would have something to say about this.

Taking a deep breath, she was glad she had gloves with her after she put them on, before picking up the scarf and putting it in the zip-lock bag. She shut it tightly, before tucking the bag into the waistband of her pants, hoping that it wouldn't slip out while she was climbing back.

She made it back out to the balcony, waving to Bastian. After she got his attention to make sure his eyes were on her, she started climbing across the rope. She felt the rope wobble, from the chair still 'anchored' to Colin's balcony starting to slide and tip over the balcony railing. She tried to climb faster, hanging on for dear life when…

The chair end of the rope fell over Colin's balcony completely, resulting in the rope descending downwards. Aubri suppressed a scream as the rope swung downwards towards Bastian's balcony, holding onto the rope for dear life, and a yelp escaped Bastian as he held on to the end he had in his hands. Aubri felt herself swing back and forth a bit, but thankfully the rope hadn't broken yet, or else she'd be falling right now.

"Shit!" Bastian grabbed onto the rope tight, trying to make sure Aubri didn't fall. Aubri gasped, looking up at Bastian, gritting her teeth briefly.

"Help me!" Aubri hissed up at Bastian, who nodded quickly, grabbing the other end of the rope tightly before pulling her up. Thankfully, the rope still didn't break, despite the strain, but after pulling Aubri onto the balcony, the two heard a soft crashing sound. Bastian looked over the balcony's railing, grimacing.

"Shit." Bastian shook his head, looking over the balcony, and then towards Aubri. "We might be in trouble."

Aubri looked up at Bastian from where she sat on the balcony floor. "What?"

"The chair. It fell."

"What!?"

"Excuse me?" Aubri overheard the familiar voice of the manager from below, only seconds later. "Is this chair yours?"

"Uh, *yeah!*" Bastian called back, leaning over the balcony just enough. The nervousness getting into his voice made Aubri want to laugh. Instead, she peered through the railing of the balcony, looking down at the manager's confused expression as Bastian continued making his excuses. "I was bringing my chair out here to enjoy the fresh air! Just, um, I just kinda tripped and it toppled over the railing before I could catch it. Sorry!"

Aubri saw the manager sigh, shaking her head before calling again. "I'll have my staff bring a new chair up to your room. You'll have to pay for damages to this one, however."

"Thanks! Sorry again!" Bastian called back, before looking towards Aubri with a relieved sigh. "Thank god we're not in too much trouble."

Aubri offered him a sheepish grin. "I'm just glad no one saw me creeping back and forth on our makeshift rope. We should probably get it untied and put back where it belongs before they get up here."

"Right. Gotta make a cover." Bastian looked down at the curtain and rope combination in his hands, then up at Aubri. "Can you make some tea and pull another chair up here while I undo all of this?"

She nodded quickly. "Got it. And I'll hide the evidence."

"Evidence?"

She offered him a sheepish grin, pointing at her pants. "I stuffed the evidence in there. I'll show you in a few moments."

By the time staff came up with a new chair, the curtain was perfectly back in place where it belonged, as well as tea freshly brewed and made, poured into cups for two. If it wasn't for the fact that they were still in the middle of investigating a murder right now, Aubi was sure she'd be more relaxed than she was right now.

"You mentioned you stuffed the evidence in your pants, right?" Bastian asked, taking a sip from his cup. "Mind showing me now?"

Aubri nodded, taking the still-bagged scarf out of her pants, and showing it to him. "Yup. This is it."

Bastian stared at the scarf, then up at Aubri. "Why couldn't you just stuff it in your pockets?"

Aubri shrugged. "I don't have deep-enough pockets as is. I had no choice but to stuff it down my pants. Besides," She tapped the bag the scarf was in, "I put it in a plastic bag beforehand. Prevent contamination, you know?"

He stiffly nodded. "Oh. That makes sense. But is it...Colin's scarf, or...?"

She swallowed, putting the scarf down on the table as she shook her head. "It belongs to Renee. I gave it to her as a birthday gift, back when we were dating...it was the last gift I got her before we broke up."

He raised a brow. "Why would Renee's scarf be in Colin's room? Do you think they were banging before he died?"

Aubri glared at him – the idea of both her exes going at it before one of them died wasn't an image she wanted in her head right now. "No! He was drunk at the time before his death. We *all* know that, so I doubt it. Even if they secretly were a thing, like you theorized, I don't think drunk sex is a great prelude to murder."

Bastian's nose wrinkled at that. "Okay, maybe they weren't banging before he died. But at the very least, we saw them fight each other, before Colin died. It's obvious that Renee is a suspect. And her scarf being in his room indicates that she had to be in there, that night."

"Fine. That's a fair possibility." Aubri didn't want to think of Renee as a suspect. It didn't make sense. Why else would she be so torn about Colin's death, especially since she already tried to leave the island as is this morning? "Renee's a suspect. But I still think she's innocent. Colin could have grabbed the scarf off her neck while fighting her before he went back to his room. We didn't get a clear shot of them fighting before we escaped with Nick after all, the other night."

"But someone did." Bastian pointed out. "The security. They have cameras in the bar and spa areas, as well as the casino area, so I'm more than sure that they have footage of Renee and Colin fighting. And same with the staff working at the bar last night. Do you think we can find them, and ask about the security footage?"

She frowned. "Will they even *let* us see the footage?"

He shrugged. "We were witnesses to the argument prior to the fighting. We might be able to persuade the staff to let us help them, if we give that excuse."

"We'd have to ask the hotel manager, Ms. Thomson, then…" Aubri frowned, recalling Renee arguing with Nessandra in the lobby. "Thomson mentioned Renee's mom, during their argument. That she owned this hotel, that is."

"Renee probably got a free vacation thanks to her. That's how she won; the contest was *rigged.*" Bastian pointed out. "Isn't that an odd coincidence? You, her ex-girlfriend, Colin, your ex-boyfriend, and Renee herself all being the winners of the contest?"

Aubri couldn't help but groan. How long was Bastian going to keep assuming that Renee was the criminal? Just because she and Colin fought didn't mean that she killed him! That was literally a red herring in the many murder mysteries she read. "It was a random selection. *You* were a random choice. She didn't even know of my former connection to you until I told her *this morning.*"

He frowned. "It still doesn't seem like a mere coincidence. That's all I'm saying."

"I know, I just…" Aubri shook her head. "Look, let's just think this through carefully. Obviously, we can't show Ms. Thomson *this,*" she held up the scarf, "because we'll get in trouble for breaking into Colin's room. But we can just say we had a speculation about someone else potentially killing Colin."

"Maybe it shouldn't be both of us asking her. It would look more believable if it's one of us asking. Or less suspicion on both of us overall, at least."

"Which one of us should ask?"

Bastian gave her a look. "You, obviously."

She frowned, brows furrowing. "Me?"

He nodded. "Yes. You are both Renee *and* Colin's ex-girlfriend. It would make sense that you're concerned for your own safety, given that it involves both of them." A hum left him, and then he chuckled. "You can deal with the security. I can try chatting up the staff from the previous night about all of this. See if there's anything I can further pry out of them."

A sigh left Aubri at that. She knew he had a point. And though he might not realize it, she did still care for Renee. She doubted she wanted to get back together with her, but that didn't mean that she and Renee couldn't at least be amiable to each other.

CHAPTER 9

Nessandra Thomson was a stoic woman, in Aubri's opinion. After initially meeting with her in her office, Aubri told her that she wanted to see the footage. She didn't change her oddly neutral expression at all as she led Aubri to the security room.

"I just think it might be possible one of the staff, or guests in the bar that night, might've killed Colin." Aubri managed, as Nessandra ordered the security to replay the footage from last night. "And…I just want to see if anyone followed him." She wasn't sure if she would see Renee following Colin out. What then?

"I see." Nessandra looked towards the security guard, who she'd asked to pull up said footage on one of the main screens in the room. "When did the fight start?"

"Started at nine-forty-five last night." The security guard muttered, as the footage began replaying. Renee appeared on the screen, as well as Colin, and Aubri felt her guts twist as the familiar argument began between those two.

"What did you say about her, you jerk!?"

"You heard me." Colin and Renee were in the standoff from last night, complete with the definitely drunk and staggering Colin. *"That piece of ass is a sugar baby, didn't you know? She's a gold digger. Bet she only dated you in high school 'cause you're rich. She just took a good look at all the expensive stuff you carried around with you, I bet, and took to you like a bear to honey! I know that you're the daughter of some big-shot company overseas. That's the only fucking reason you got that internship after highschool! Not surprised she dated you."*

"Liar." Renee looked scandalized; eyes wide as she blanched. *"You're lying!"*

Aubri swallowed as she watched the conversation ensue, getting more and more aggressive. She tried not to think much of how Renee would or could possibly kill Colin. She knew Renee's temper could when she wanted it to, and her fight with Colin was a good example of that. But did that mean she was the killer?

Colin raised his voice, trying to gesture in Aubri's direction as Aubri and Bastian were already leaving, *"She's a slut for money, Renee! She's always been some slut! She was sugaring behind my back!"*

Renee hissed, before punching Colin hard in the face, hard enough for him to stagger back. *"You fucking liar! Stop insulting my ex-girlfriend, you asshole!!"*

Several of the crowd backed up when Colin punched Renee back, before both grappled with each other for several seconds. Renee managed to even push Colin into the table, just as Colin ripped the scarf off Renee's neck.

That was when security barged towards Renee and Colin, one of them yelling *"Break it up!"* Colin and Renee yelled insults and slurs at each other as they were dragged out of the bar, while one of the bartenders got to work trying to calm the otherwise shocked crowds.

"Ms. Harlow?" Aubri looked towards Nessandra, who frowned. "As far as I'm seeing, this video footage only gives stronger evidence against Ms. Renee Dimitri. Is there anyone else you recognize in that crowd that could have killed Colin?"

Aubri shook her head, a sigh leaving her. More evidence, against *Renee* of all people? Surely someone else in this hotel had to have a grudge on Colin, right? She was sure anyone could be mad at Colin for ruining the mood at the bar and causing a fight. Then again, that didn't make sense to have murder ensue.

"No." She admitted. She didn't want to admit it, but there was no one else that looked suspicious. Nothing that caught her attention other than the fight between Renee and Colin. "But thanks, for trying."

Nessandra looked towards Aubri sympathetically, with a soft frown of her own. "If you think of anyone else suspicious, please let me know immediately. Just call the front desk and ask for me."

"Thank you, Ms. Thomson. I appreciate the help." Aubri took a deep breath, turning on her heel to leave the security room. She heard Thomson clear her throat, and Aubri looked back towards her, noticing that Nessandra's expression changed to worried, furrowed brows.

"And please," Nessandra managed, "Be careful. If I were you, I'd get back to your room immediately. Tonight's curfew is approaching."

Aubri nodded. "I will."

She left the security room with a heavy heart, hoping that what she saw wasn't true.

As Aubri walked down the hallway, she heard Renee's voice.

"Aubri?"

She turned to see Renee approach her, taking a deep breath. "I saw walk into the security room earlier. What was that about?"

"You did?" Aubri's heart skipped a beat. She'd hoped that no one would see her enter the security room unnoticed. How was she supposed to cover this up? There was no way she could just say she walked into that room by accident or give any excuse. She had no choice but to tell the truth.

"Are you okay?" Renee frowned, swallowing. "What's going on, Aubri?"

'Yeah, I'm fine, uh…" Aubri scratched the back of her head, before looking Renee in the eye. "I just thought, maybe I might catch a glimpse of Colin's killer if I saw the footage from the bar. When you and Colin were fighting."

"I didn't see anyone follow him." Renee cut in almost too quickly, shaking her head.

"Yeah, but maybe someone else did after you weren't looking. I don't know." Aubri shrugged. "I'm still trying to figure it out."

Renee's frown remained, and Aubri noticed her brows furrow. "Is it worth it? What if it puts *you* in danger?"

"I'm trying to keep this discreet." Aubri looked her in the eye. She decided it was best not to tell Renee that she already risked her life, this morning, when sneaking into Colin's room. "Don't tell anyone, okay?"

She nodded. "I won't. Promise."

Aubri paused; the question stuck in her throat. It would help her get information, but still...could she bear Renee's reaction? She decided to risk it, anyway. After all, nothing would get done if she didn't ask the right questions at the right time. "What did you do, Renee? After you and Colin fought?"

A sigh left her ex-girlfriend as she flicked a few strands of dark hair out of her face. "I went straight to my hotel room after walking out the alcohol in my system. I went down to the beach, then back into the hotel, and then went straight to my room and got some sleep. That's it. Next thing I know, I woke up and Colin's dead."

Aubri went quiet, taking a deep breath. A relieved breath left her. "So...you're not the killer, then. That's good."

"What?" Renee sounded suddenly hoarse. She looked up at her ex-girlfriend's face, eyes widening in horror. "Do you think that *I* killed him?"

Aubri cursed herself, shaking her head. "No, no, not me!"

Renee's brows furrowed, and her voice darkened as she

asked, "Your *friend?*"

"Not him, either!" Aubri shook her head. The last time she heard Renee be this borderline angry, it was during her fight with Colin before he died! "I, uh, overheard some rumours! From the other guests!"

Renee raised a brow, the rage in her gaze softening. "The other guests?" She repeated.

"Yeah." Aubri suddenly hoped she didn't sentence an innocent person to death because of it. "Because you and Colin had that fight before he died, and they were all there to witness it."

"Oh, that." Renee winced, her voice softening. "Well...I suppose that makes sense. I'm not surprised. But..." She took a deep breath, looking Aubri in the eyes. "Thank you. For telling me. Stay safe, okay?"

Aubri nodded. "I will. You do the same, too."

Aubri watched Renee leave, and she swallowed, feeling her heart sink deep into her chest as she went to check in on Bastian and see how he was doing. If Renee wasn't the killer, who was it?

CHAPTER 10

Aubri heard the sound of vomiting as she approached Bastian's room. She knocked on it, before calling.

"Bastian!? It's Aubri!"

"Aubri!?" She heard him yelp from inside. "Get the fuck in here! I might be poisoned!"

"What the hell!?" She dashed into the room to see the bathroom door open, followed by the sounds of puking. She grimaced at the smell, before carefully approaching the bathroom, knowing Bastian had to be in there. He held his own head over the toilet, gripping the edges of the seat for dear life before a slow groan left him. He turned, wiping the back of his mouth with a grimace as he noticed her.

"Remember how I mentioned that I would chat up the staff a bit?" Bastian managed, his voice hoarse. "Well…Nick joined me for a little impromptu lunch date. Served me one of those winners' drinks as he promised. But…"

"But?" She prompted, swallowing. Bastian looked horribly pale right now. "Are you….?"

"Think he might've poisoned me." Another groan left him as he struggled to stand, and she quickly helped him do so. "And I think he might've poisoned Colin, too."

"Poison?" She repeated. She thought of all the murder mysteries where poison was involved. The only person that served winners' drinks to her and Bastian was Nick, right? "Do you think Nick also served Colin that night, when he died?" She could imagine it now; Colin, standing on the balcony, suddenly coughing up blood before falling over the railing due to the poison in his system from all the drinks he had. It would certainly explain how he fell to his death, for sure, and he *had* been heavily drunk the night died. It could be a slow-acting poison, Aubri guessed.

"Possibly. I mean, Nick was the only one serving us winners' drinks, right? Can't think of who else it would be!" Bastian swallowed lightly, only for him to gag, nose wrinkling. As he stumbled over to the sink to rinse his mouth, Aubri grimaced, flushing the toilet to get rid of the vomited-up shit in there.

"If that's the case," She breathed as she looked towards him, "what do we do?"

"I have his *actual* number," Bastian rasped after he finished rinsing his mouth. "On my phone, since he was *so* nice to leave it when he first called my room. You can call him now and get him up here."

"Shouldn't we report this to security first!? Or get you a medic!?"

"He might be the only one who has an antidote!" Bastian whimpered, still lying on the floor. "Negotiate with the enemy to let us live and in return, we live. If we just straight-up try to get him arrested or something, he might just try to off both of us. It's a classic trend in a couple books I read recently!"

Aubri sighed. Bastian had a point – negotiating with the culprit often happened in confrontations. She grabbed Bastian's phone from him after he offered it to her, before finding Nick's number, calling him.

"Hello?" It was Nick on the other end, and a soft, carefree chuckle left him. *"Bastian, I just finished another shift. What's up?"*

"This isn't Bastian." Aubri answered sharply. "It's Aubri. What the hell did you do with him?"

"Aubri!?" She heard Nick gasp. *"Why are you calling through Bastian's phone? Is he okay?"*

"He's barfing into the toilet, Nick, and he's *not* okay. Did you poison Bastian and Colin? And by the way, you're on speaker."

If Aubri could see Nick right now, she imagined his jaw dropping. *"Okay, what!? Why am I accused of murder now?"*

"Bastian was throwing up when I found him, just after his date with you." She pointed out, raising a brow. "Fess up, will you?"

"I didn't put anything in his or Colin's drinks!" Aubri could hear Nick borderline stammering, *"I don't even know how to poison anyone!"*

"Then why is he ill!?"

"I don't know!" The other's voice leaked worry and horror at once. Aubri suddenly had the gut feeling that she was approaching this situation wrong, as Nick continued. *"I only served him one drink before I was put on break. We only had water after that drink, during our date."*

"It's *true.*" Aubri heard Bastian groan in the background. She heard Nick sigh, before speaking up again.

"I think I know what did it, though. The food."

"What?" That hadn't been the answer Aubri expected.

Nick simply sighed. *"Yes. His burger might've been undercooked before serving it."*

If that was the case, and Bastian threw up because of it, was it...food poisoning? Aubri wasn't sure whether she should be relived or more horrified. "Why the *hell* did you serve him an undercooked burger?"

"We were in a rush to put out orders for lunch, right before my shift ended. Bastian was the last person I served before my shift was officially over and I joined him for lunch. And if you don't believe me, ask Lisa, because she was still on her shift when mine ended."

Aubri sighed. At least she knew that her friend wasn't about to die of actual poison in the next few hours. "At least that explains things…" At least she didn't have to worry about a second attempted murder right now.

"I *thought* my burger was a little on the cold side." Bastian muttered, shaking his head lightly. "I should've checked before eating the whole damn thing…"

Aubri overheard Nick sigh. *"Sorry for food-poisoning you, handsome. And I'm sorry if this leads to us not seeing each other anymore."*

A brief chuckle left Bastian as he looked towards Nick. "Well, I'm sorry for me and Aubri accusing you of murder – both attempted and succeeded. I think we're even this time around."

"So," Aubri looked between the phone and Bastian, "This means Colin wasn't poisoned before he died?"

"No." Nick managed, and Aubri heard him sigh. *"I remember seeing Colin that night - he was just really drunk. The thing is, he didn't order anything to eat that night. He only wanted drinks, so I served him about three in total. I tried to slow down serving him any more drinks or offered him water in between, after that, but I think he must've called another bartender to serve him while I wasn't looking…"*

"All that probably happened while Nick was serving *us*, then." Bastian muttered, looking towards Aubri. Aubri tried to imagine it in her head; Nick serving up winners' drinks for Colin, before being called to prepare two for Aubri and Bastian, giving Colin enough time to call over another bartender to serve him something else…

"Hence him getting so drunk that he got into a fight with Renee that night?" Aubri finished.

Nick hummed lightly, before answering. *"Yup. That's why I offered to get you two out of there. I didn't know that either of you knew him, but I did know that I didn't want any of the other contest winners being involved in that fight for sure. It's my fault he got drunk that night – though my coworkers were nice enough not to rat me out to management when they heard about what happened. Maybe if I'd made sure that he didn't get more alcohol for sure, then..."* A slow sigh left him, after. *"I'm sorry. I told all of this to security, but I should have told both of you sooner."*

Aubri could tell that Nick sounded genuinely guilty; his tone of voice cracked at the last sentence. Nick hadn't poisoned Colin's drink while he wasn't looking with any fatal drugs, which was for sure. Responsible for actual food poisoning, but at least it was accidental.

"I believe you." Aubri managed. "Sorry to badger you so much so early in the morning."

"It's okay." A weak chuckle left the other. "I can understand why you got so worried, given everything going on."

"Just to clarify," Bastian managed, "Were you the *only* one that made the winners' drinks for all of us winners?"

"Yeah. I made the recipe myself, actually!" Nick chuckled. *"Since there were only four of you winners, and I was on shift every night for this week at least, all the winners' drink-making duties are on me."*

So, the winners' drinks weren't poisoned unless one of the other bartenders had a serious grudge towards Colin for whatever reason, and Aubri doubted that. Colin hadn't been poisoned that night, so that possibility was fully eliminated based on everything she and Bastian now knew.

"Do you want me to get someone to send any meds or antibiotics up here?" Nick asked. *"You know, to make up for the food poisoning."*

"I'm usually pretty fine after a few hours of vomiting, but some medicine would honestly help me right now." Bastian called. He paused, before asking, "Would it be legally possible for you to deliver it yourself, or is that asking too much of me?"

"Unfortunately, I have another shift scheduled later today, so I can't – but I can get one of the other hotel staff to deliver meds." A sigh

left Nick at that statement. *"But I would be happy to make it up to you some other time."*

Aubri heard Bastian chuckle at that. "I'll hold you to your word."

"Don't worry," Aubri heard Nick laugh. "I'm good at that."

"Now that we have that resolved…" Aubri looked towards Bastian, offering him a light grin. "Just rest, okay? And no more drinks until you're better."

Bastian sighed, leaning back against the closest wall as he closed his eyes. "That's a shame. I would *love* to drown my sorrows right now."

"Is there anything else you need me to do?" Nick asked. *"Anything I should watch out for?"*

"Just don't die." Bastian spoke up. "Okay? I'd like to see your face in-person and not in a murder case. And I'd also rather not see you dead, either."

"I'll do my best. I got to get freshened up before my shift this evening, so I need to hang up. See you soon." With that, Nick hung up.

Aubri sighed, looking up at Bastian from the phone, before handing it back to him. "Sorry about all of that. I just thought…"

"No, it's fine. I'm the one who brought up him possibly being a murderer, anyway. But at least we know it's not him." Bastian offered her a weak grin, as he shook his head. "Look, I'm honestly exhausted and I'm not going to get much done here…not that I can think of, anyway."

"And I talked to security, and we have nothing of use." Aubri muttered, shaking her head. "I didn't see anyone who visibly followed Colin out of the bar after his fight with Renee. He *did* rip off her scarf during the fight, though, which explains why it was there in his room when he was murdered. He must've taken it with him."

"Really?" Bastian frowned lightly at that. "Well, I suppose

that explains things."

She sighed. "You still think Renee did it, didn't you?"

"I know it's annoying you that I'm so suspicious of her, but…" He started, but Aubri frowned, her brows furrowing as she shook her head.

"I talked to her firsthand when I bumped into her, just after checking out security. She just went straight to her room and got some sleep. I presume she wanted to get her scarf back if she could, but…there's nothing indicating she was in Colin's room that night, given her testimony." Aubri cut in before Bastian could finish. "Besides, her scarf was still in Colin's room when I snuck in, and *he* was the one who grabbed it off her in the first place."

"But why didn't she just ask security to help her?" Bastian stated, tilting his head to the side. "Especially if her mother owns this resort? She easily could have complained to management!"

"She was more concerned about her own safety! Remember?" She tried her best not to groan. "We saw her begging to go home, literally the morning after the murder happened."

"Aubri–" He started, but then he moved to the toilet, dry-heaving once. A groan left him as he looked up at her, shaking his head. "I think I need to rest up before I can even argue with you, any further. Okay?"

Aubri sighed. Bastian had a point. It wouldn't help him get any better, and she had a lot to process herself, from confronting Renee and Nick to seeing the security tapes. If the killer wasn't in a rush to pursue any new targets, she and Bastian could wait until the next day to figure things out, right?

CHAPTER 11

The next day came, and Aubri woke up to her cellphone ringing. She quickly answered it, sitting up in bed as she did so. "Hello?"

"Aubri?" It was Bastian speaking. *"It's me. Morning."*

"Bastian? How are you feeling?"

"A lot better. Sucked on a couple ice chips from the freezer, drank a lot of water, and ate a fuck-ton of crackers before sleeping. While I was resting up, though, I found something on Renee. You need to check it out. Come to my room as soon as you can, okay?"

"What is it about Renee that you found?"

"Just get to my room first. I think it's best we discuss this in-person. And don't worry," A sheepish chuckle left him, *"I won't vomit all over you, I promise."*

It only took fifteen minutes for Aubri to get dressed and run over to Bastian's room, and less than ten seconds for him to open the door for her and let him in.

"So, Aubri started, looking towards Bastian as he shut the door behind them. Bastian had gotten dressed neatly as if he'd never been food-poisoned in the first place, though Aubri figured that he was just trying to be strong for his and her own sakes. "How did you find stuff on Renee, exactly?"

"Internet, obviously." A sigh left him, gesturing to his laptop. "The wi-fi still works in here, despite all the murders. There are other guests complaining online about being stuck on the island while waiting for the police and so on, so...I can't imagine this place staying open for long after the murder, unless they capitalize on it or something." His nose wrinkled at that, and he shook his head. "Anyway, as I was saying earlier, I found some things about Renee that might...be of concern, to you."

Aubri felt her chest tighten as she followed him to the laptop he had set up on the desk. "What things did you find on Renee?"

"Let's see..." He looked down at the laptop screen, then up at Aubri, frowning. "She stalked a girl that looks quite similar to you."

"Really?" *Renee? Stalk someone? She'd never do that, would she?* Renee had never been overly aggressive to her, back when they dated. Sure, she recalled how Renee pleaded for the chance to get back together with her, the day after Colin died, but she was just reacting fearfully, right?

He turned the laptop towards her, showing her. "Read it and find out. Maybe it was a good thing you broke up with Renee after high school, after all."

Aubri didn't say a word, reading the news on the laptop. What she saw of it made her go silent.

Billionaire's daughter guilty of stalking, attempted assault, and harassment

Renee Dimitri, age 25, daughter of Rita Dimitri, owner of Paradiso Networks, has been found guilty of stalking, attempted assaulting and harassing Aria Hawthorn, age 24. Dimitri and Hawthorn formerly dated, and Hawthorn reports that Dimitri stalked her since three months ago after they separated.

After repeated activity of harassment, stalking and attempted assault during the two months after the breakup, Hawthorn pressed charges towards Dimitri for her crimes. Dimitri, arrested only a month ago, has been found guilty yesterday, and is sentenced to pay up to $5000 and spend attend Crown appointed psychological sessions, effective immediately.

Aubri checked the date of the article, frowning. "This was

only published two months ago."

"Which means she probably *just* finished carrying out her sentence. Probably wanted a vacation to get away from all of this, hence why she's here. But I don't feel right about all of this." Bastian looked up at Aubri, gritting his teeth. "Aubri, your ex recently stalked another ex of hers before, and now it's possible she's killed Colin because of you. Don't you think it might be her?"

Aubri shook her head. "That can't be true."

"Aubri…" He started, but Aubri glared at him.

"She would never stalk her. I mean, I know she's rich. I *guess* her hiring people to stalk her is possible, but what if her ex just took advantage of the breakup? Spun things in her favour?" Aubri knew that was a trend that happened in some mystery novels. What if that was happening right now? Even with this information Bastian found about Renee, it didn't necessarily mean that she'd murder anyone, would she?

A groan escaped Bastian at that as he pointed towards the screen. "Aubri, think about what you're saying–"

"Bastian," She cut in, gritting her teeth, "I *know* what I'm talking about. It *can't* be her!"

"Just…" Bastian took a deep breath, then stopped, shaking his head. A sigh left him at that, and then he looked down at the laptop, then up at her. "If you don't believe me, then fine. You can deny how I feel about it if that's what you want. But you can't deny *facts.* The *fact* is that your ex-girlfriend stalked one of her own exes before. Whether it pins her as a potential suspect, well…we both know that it's obvious she is one. Even if it turns out she's not the murderer, we can't just *not* suspect her. Not after learning what we know so far."

The phone suddenly rang. Bastian picked it up quickly. "Hello?"

Aubri watched Bastian go pale, and he swallowed. "Uh, yeah. Thanks…for letting me know." He took a deep breath, putting down the phone.

Aubri looked up at him. "What is it?"

Bastian looked towards her. "Apparently, according to Ms. Thomson, the guards in the security room were just found murdered. All the footage of everything that happened at the bar, during the night of the murder, was stolen."

CHAPTER 12

The security tapes were *stolen?*

The guards —*murdered?*

Aubri lay in bed in her own room. She needed time to let all this news sink in and retreated to her own room to try to sleep through it after Bastian told her what happened, to process. First, Colin was murdered. Now, security guards were murdered *and* the camera footage of what happened at the bar was missing. Nessandra guessed, according to Bastian, that the records were copied onto a USB by the killer or deleted entirely to avoid having incriminating evidence.

But who would break into the security room so easily? Was it an inside job? Aubri didn't sleep a wink, with all the thoughts running through her mind. A sigh left her as she sat up in bed, reading the clock on the nearby bedtable. 6 a.m. *I'm going to need some strong coffee…and maybe a few drinks.*

As she sat up to get refreshed and get ready for the day, knowing that trying to sleep was futile at this point, she remembered Nessandra and Renee's argument the morning after Colin was murdered.

"I'm calling my mom about this. She's going to be pissed to find out I'm stuck on the same island as the murderer!"

"I'm sure your mother would be likely to agree with keeping you and the other guests safe from the murderer, with these precautions in place, as well as keeping that murderer from escaping justice."

A horrible, awful idea occurred in Aubri's mind. What if Renee *was* the one that stole the information from the bar? She'd seen Renee outside of the security office when walking out, the other day. Renee knew where it was. She could easily make it back to the security office later and try to take the recorded video involving her and Colin…

What if Bastian was right? What if it's really her? Had her past love, and current care for Renee really deceive her to the truth this whole time? Was *that* why Renee tried to get back together with Aubri shortly after Colin's death, to cover up murdering Colin? A pit formed in her stomach as she sat up in bed. She thought about the article Bastian showed her.

She stalked someone that looked exactly like me. If that's what she did to a stranger that looked like me, what would she do if I didn't get back together with her?

Of course, even if Renee did stalk someone that looked like her and wanted to get back together with her, that wasn't proof alone that she killed Colin, was it? It was enough to creep Aubri out of getting back together with her, though. And sure, the scarf she found in Colin's room was a piece of evidence. However, the security footage being stolen meant that there wouldn't be enough evidence to incriminate Renee. But if Aubri had that security footage for the police to see, then…

What if I sneak into her room and find out for myself?

Aubri knew this was probably a bad idea. But sneaking into Renee's room and trying to see if she had any evidence of her killing Colin sounded like the best idea, if she wanted to find out if Renee killed Colin for sure. Any murderer would want to hide past connections with their victims, after all; that was yet another common trend she recognized in the books she read. There was no way hotel staff would just snoop into others' materials during room service, so Aubri figured that she had to do it herself. Besides, security guards were already dead for doing their job. What if it was an innocent guest that got murdered, next?

Aubri took a deep breath, got dressed and out of bed, before going over to Bastian's room. She knocked on the door, and as

Bastian opened it to see her, she looked him in the eye and spoke. No more hiding from the truth. No more letting her past love for Renee deceive her.

"I need to break into Renee's room. And I need you to help me."

"What?" Bastian's eyes widened, but before he could ask further, Aubri swallowed.

"I'm sorry I didn't believe you earlier. I should've trusted you, because...I think you're right. She might be the murderer. And..." She leaned forwards, her head touching his shoulder. "I'm sorry for not believing you."

"Aubri." She felt his chest rise and fall as he sighed, before wrapping a gentle arm around her. He'd comforted her like this, once, after she ended their fake-dating arrangement and after she broke up with Colin. It was nice. It was needed. "How about I get you some coffee first, and then we'll talk this plan through carefully? If she's the murderer for sure, then this could get dangerous quick."

She nodded, looking up at him to see that gentle gaze at his, and for a moment, she felt a calmness take over her – the first time she felt this way since Colin's death a few days earlier. "I think I'd like that."

CHAPTER 13

After both ate breakfast first (they ordered room service) and got appropriately changed, they decided: Aubri would break into Renee's room by doing the same balcony trick as they did with breaking into Colin's room, earlier in the week. The problem was that Bastian's balcony was not parallel to Renee's room. Aubri's room was, however, so they set up the same rope-and-chair technique as they did last time, except from Aubri's room.

"What if Renee comes back?" Aubri asked, looking towards Bastian as she securely tied the makeshift rope's end to the chair.

"I saw her leave her room, earlier." Bastian managed, looking towards Renee's balcony, and then back at Aubri. "I overheard her talking on her phone about going to the beach when she left about half an hour ago. Also, room service already left her room a minute ago. You won't walk in on cleaning staff if that's what you're worried about."

"O...kay." Aubri raised a brow. "How did you find all of that out?"

He sighed. "I took a peek outside the door, while you were preparing the rope in your own room."

"Did she see you? Did you mention anything about the case to her at all?" Aubri asked.

"No. I didn't even talk to her. She seemed like she was in a hurry, so she never noticed me even seeing her." He hesitated, then asked, "Did you talk to her at all, recently?"

"She spotted me outside the security room, the other day, after I went to see the security footage of the fight between her and Colin." Aubri confessed, frowning. "I had to tell her that I was simply trying to help the guards spot who might have potentially killed Colin. I didn't say it was her, but *she* thought I was accusing her of it."

"Oof." He grimaced, shaking his head. "Sorry to hear that."

"Thanks...." Aubri held up the newly made rope and curtain combination they once used to get onto Colin's balcony. "Ready to break in?"

He smiled. "I'm ready."

Getting across both balconies with the chair as an anchor worked as smoothly as it did last time; with Aubri climbing over the rope with using her hands and ankles for guidance to stay on as she made her way to the other side. She opened the balcony doors, shutting them behind her, and looked around.

Renee's hotel room was identical to her own; the bathroom was clear and neat, likely due to room service having just left, and the living room was spotless. Upon checking the bedroom, however, Aubri noticed Renee's laptop on the bedtable. It was plugged into the wall, probably charging from earlier use. If she wanted to keep records of security footage, it was likely on there, or a USB. At least she'd brought her own to just copy the files on. She'd intended to use it in case to save some of her own vacation photos on, but those plans changed since Colin's murder.

She opened and turned the laptop on, hoping to find the information she desired. However, she found herself stuck at the login section. Aubri frowned. What password would Renee use?

She said she missed me. What if she used my own name?

She plugged in 'A-U-B-R-I' as the password, and it surprisingly worked. She wasn't sure if she should feel good about that, or not. As she surveyed the desktop on the screen, however, she soon noticed that there were files on the computer. Upon opening it, she saw the videos from…the bar.

From *that* night.

"She's a slut for money, Renee! She's always been some slut! She was sugaring behind my back!"

Aubri watched Renee hiss back at Colin in the video, before punching him hard in the face, hard enough for him to stagger back. *"You fucking liar! Stop insulting my ex-girlfriend, you asshole !"*

Aubri quickly closed the video, before taking out the USB from her pocket. Could she copy the videos onto this? It could work, right? She took a deep breath, plugging in the USB, before copying all the videos on. She checked the desktop further for anything else and found a whole file about herself.

Aubri swallowed. These photos of her *weren't* just from high school. Some of them looked like herself, during her time at uni. There were even a few photos snapped of her with Colin! Her stomach twisted as she recalled the article Bastian shared with her, about Renee supposedly stalking another ex-girlfriend of hers. Did Renee hire people to stalk *her*, too?

What if she knows about me and Bastian's past? She examined all the photos on the laptop for any sign of Bastian, but she didn't see anything. A relieved sigh left her. *At least she doesn't know about him. Would she try murdering him after Colin if she did?*

There was another file among Aubri's photos on the desktop, and Aubri clicked on it to open a few emails, sent between Nessandra and Renee. The latest email read the following:

Dear Ms. Dimitri,

Ms. Harlow has been selected as one of the winners of the contest, and she has confirmed that she'll be coming to Calloway Resort in the upcoming month. I hope your mother is ready to pay extra fees to secure your win. This better be worth you getting your sweetheart back.

Aubri swallowed. *Nessandra helped her?*

Does she know about the murders, or does she only have a hand in Renee coming to this hotel because of me? She had to ask, later. Right now, she had to finish copying these files into her USB and get out of here as fast as she could. She quickly turned off the laptop after she took out the USB post-copying the items. She turned, about to run back to Renee's balcony so she could make it back to her own room with the found evidence, when she tripped, hitting the ground. A groan left her as she got up, clutching the bedtable, but she accidentally grabbed the drawer, pulling it open. As she got up, she noticed two guns inside the bedtable drawer. *Why does Renee have guns here? Did she kill Colin with them?*

Is that how he died? She shot him and then threw him off the balcony? She quickly shut the drawer, shaking her head. There hadn't been word of any bullet lodged in his head, or else she might've heard of that from the security staff. *But a gun is still heavy enough to hit someone in the head, right? And if she pushed him off the balcony to cover up the initial impact, then...*

Aubri tried to imagine it in the back of her mind; a drunk Colin turning around, only to be hit in the head with the blunt end of a gun. Renee, dragging his flailing body to the balcony and pushing him over the railing, probably trying to land it in the pool, only to miss and hit the paved deck instead. Either landing would kill him. Even if he did survive the initial fall, by landing in the pool rather than the paved deck, he would be too drunk and injured from the initial head wound to swim to safety.

It made sense; Aubri supposed. Amid the loud partying and music late into the night, *no one* would hear one man getting pushed off a balcony so easily, especially if they were all drunk and out of their minds. A perfect cover for a murder.

All she knew was that, right now, she had to make it back to her own room and let Bastian know what she found. Maybe he could help her. At this point, she wasn't sure who else to trust but him.

CHAPTER 14

"Are you okay?"

"Yes, Bastian. I'm fine." Aubri took a deep breath, holding up the USB as Bastian managed to get both the chair end of the rope off Renee's balcony, pulling it up quickly before the chair could fall off and hit the pool deck below from the weight like last time. "Renee stole the security files. Also, she has guns hidden in her room."

"What?" Bastian blanched at that as he went straight into the living room. Aubri followed him back into the living room area of the hotel room. "Why does she have *guns?*"

"Probably to kill Colin." Aubri finally managed, looking up at him. "I'm pretty sure she murdered Colin – Not by shooting him, but she hit him in the head with one of the guns. They looked small, but they're heavy enough to pick up. Also, she and the manager, Thomson, rigged the contest so that Renee would also win the contest if *I* won, after I confirmed post-winning that I was coming to the hotel. They exchanged emails before all of us came to this resort."

"So, even the *manager* is in on the whole murder?" His jaw dropped. "Look, I've read my share of mysteries, but *this* is a plot twist I wasn't expecting. Is she even aware that she helped give Renee an opportunity to murder Colin?"

"I don't know. She didn't say in the email that she knew that Renee was going to murder him. All she knew was that the contest was rigged so Renee could try to *win me back.*" Aubri stressed, swallowing. She felt that sick feeling in the pit of her stomach return, and she did her best to ignore it. "And I don't know how I can find evidence of whether Nessandra is in on this, other than her just up and telling me. I might have no choice but to ask her. Maybe…" She paused, then looked up at him. "I could lie, maybe? Claim I heard a rumor or two that the contest was rigged? That might be safer."

"That's possible." Bastian gestured to the room's phone. "Be my guest. Go ahead and use my phone if you want to ask her."

"Thanks." Aubri quickly picked up the phone, dialing the front desk's number before putting the phone on speaker so both she and Bastian would hear the other end of the line.

"Calloway Resort," the main desk staff answered. *"How may we help you?"*

"May I speak with the manager, Ms. Thomson, please? It's an emergency."

"One moment, please." There was a beep, and then a new voice spoke up.

"Nessandra Thomson, how may I help you?"

"Ms. Thomson? This is Aubri." Aubri took a deep breath. "I, uh, heard a rumour that you rigged the contest so that Renee Dimitri could come here, since her mom owns the hotel. Is that true?"

She heard Thomson gasp, just slightly, but then a sigh left her.

"I suppose I have no choice but to say it. I did, yes." Aubri could tell, from her tone, that she sounded hesitant, but her hushed tones indicated guilt. *" It was a favour on her mother's behalf, after she gave me the position of hotel manager. Renee wanted to get back together with you, so after I found out that you entered the contest, she immediately wanted to be a winner along with you."*

"What about the other two winners?"

Another sigh left Thomson at that question. *"I didn't know of Colin being your ex until after his murder. And as far as I know,*

Bastian is unrelated to any of you." She paused, before continuing. *"Also, the police just contacted me less than an hour ago. They should be here within the next hour, as the weather cleared up on their end."*

"Really?" Aubri decided it was best not to mention that Bastian was her former classmate and former fake-boyfriend to Nessandra. *So, Bastian's win was an actual coincidence. Huh.* "Well, uh...thanks. For letting me know. I appreciate it." At least the police would be here soon, she told herself. She paused, looking down at the USB in her spare hand, and then took a deep breath as she heard Nessandra speak up again.

"You are welcome, Miss Harlow." Nessandra paused, before asking, *"Is there anything else you found about who could possibly be the murderer? I have staff asking some of the other guests, as well, but they've come up with nothing."*

Aubri swallowed. Should she let Nessandra know her thoughts on who the murderer was? It was only fair, given how much Nessandra helped her so far, she decided. Might as well let the cat out of the bag, especially with the police coming soon.

"The thing is," Aubri finally confessed, "I think I know now who killed Colin. It's Renee."

She heard the older woman gasp. *"What? How did you...?"*

"She's the one that killed the security guards and took the footage from the bar, too." Aubri explained quickly. "I copied it from her laptop onto a spare USB I have if you want to see the evidence for yourself. Renee also has guns in her room, too. I think she snuck them in with her luggage."

"How did you find that unless...?" Nessandra started, then cleared her throat. *"I'm not going to ask questions about that right now. Is this true? You have actual evidence?"*

"Yes." She swallowed. "I can bring it to you, discreetly. Is that okay?"

"Well..." Nessandra started, but there was a pause. Aubri frowned, trying listen carefully, in case Nessandra lowered her

voice to a complete whisper on the other end.

That was when Aubri heard a gasp, and then a gunshot. Footsteps echoed from the other end of the line followed by Renee's voice. *"Aubri? Is that you on the phone?"*

Aubri didn't answer, quiet. She heard Renee chuckle, before speaking up again. *"I know you went into my room. You must really want me back if you did so, right? Don't worry, sweetheart. I'll be right upstairs when I can. I just need to..."* She heard the click of a gun, *"Get some people out of the way, first. We've got too many witnesses, after all. And since the manager knows, that means I must kill the staff, right? And all the guests, hm?"*

"Security!" Someone was heard screaming, but that was when several more gunshots resounded, followed by a low, long tone.

Aubri slammed the phone down, forcing herself to exhale the breath she held. What should she do? Run? Get help? Was Nessandra even alive? Did Renee just *kill* her?

Bastian looked towards Aubri as Aubri quickly hung up, frowning. "What happened? I heard something banging at the end of that call..."

She swallowed, looking him in the eye. "It's Renee. She knows we snuck into her room. She's shooting up the whole place and plans to get me!"

"What?" Bastian paled, staggering back slightly. He shook his head, voice growing hoarse. "Shooting up the place? As in... she's killing *everyone* here?"

"Yeah." She nodded. "That banging you heard was her shooting at Nessandra or some security guard. Can't figure out which one."

"Oh, *god.*" He shook his head again, before looking up at Aubri, eyes bulging as his shoulders grew rigid. [CL1]"Nick is on his shift right now! He wouldn't know until it's too late. I need to get down there and make sure he's safe!"

She shook her head, grabbing him by the wrist before he could move towards the door. "You'll be in the line of fire if you do that! What if Renee spots you!?"

He shook his arm out of her grip, shaking his head quickly. "Nick doesn't know *anything* about Renee having guns, or her being involved in any of this case. He and everyone else in this resort are in danger! The police aren't even arriving for at least another hour. I must do *something*, Aubri!"

"The security guards did bust in when Renee tried to shoot Nessandra. Maybe they stopped her...?" Aubri started, but then she frowned, remembering how the previous security guards were killed. No, it was more likely that Renee killed them by now. If she could kill her drunk ex-boyfriend and a few security guards without guns, she could probably kill everyone possible at this resort.

A gunshot echoed from outside, then more. The sounds of screaming outside elicited a visible shudder from Bastian before he looked towards Aubri and shoved his keycard into her hand. "Take this."

"What?" She looked down at the key card, and then up at him, seeing him move towards the door.

"You stay hidden until the police come, so you can pass the evidence to them. Hide in my room if you must. I'm going to make sure Nick's safe!"

"Bastian!"

It was too late. Bastian ran out the door and closed it behind him. Aubri knew that chasing him was pointless. He was too much like her, in Aubri's opinion; once he had his mind set on something, it was hard to stop him. Especially when it came to protecting the people he cared for.

She took a deep breath, trying to think clearly despite the sounds of screaming and gunshots outside. Nessandra's office and the security room was on the second floor of the hotel. Right now,

Aubri herself was on the top floor. Aubri knew by now that the elevator was fast. It wouldn't take long for Renee to get to her, after shooting as many people as possible down below. Bastian's right, Aubri realized. It was too dangerous to confront Renee head-on and much better to hide, especially if the police were on the way. Aubri knew she was a great climber, but she stood no chance against Renee armed with guns.

Bullets continued firing as screams followed. Aubri looked towards the window, then looked towards the door leading out of her suite. Could she run? Could she get out of her, amidst the chaos, and hide in the beach area until the police came?

Or was it too risky? Even if she tried to just leave the building, there was too much of a risk of running into Renee during her shooting rampage. Staying hidden would be the best-case scenario, then.

What about Bastian? Her blood froze as she thought of him. *He's probably at on the main floor right now, trying to save Nick. What if he's dead? What if she found him and shot him already?* She hoped he wasn't dead.

The murder mysteries that I've read mention, often, about the detectives getting into dangerous situations. How do I get out of this one?

The answer came to her instantly: She *had* to hide in Bastian's room. Renee would probably search Aubri's room immediately once she made it to this floor. As she considered the option, she also remembered that Renee also knew, by now, that Bastian was close to Aubri. Renee would just search Bastian's room next if she couldn't find Aubri in her own room.

What about Colin's room? Aubri realized, and a chill ran down her spine. *What if I hid in there? No one would bother searching the room of a dead guy, right? I don't think Renee would want to.*

She needed to go to Colin's room for her own safety. *Now.*

She ran outside of her own suite, after making a makeshift

dummy out of her bedroom's pillows and put them in her bed, making it look like she was sleeping in there. She then closed her own room door, locking it, before going over to Colin's room, trying to open it.

The door was shut and locked. A curse left her, before she looked towards Bastian's room door, and then down at the key card in her hand. Bastian gave her the spare key card – could she go into Bastian's room, cross the balcony on her own to Colin's room, and then hide in there?

She slid the key card into the lock, and the door to Bastian's room unlocked with a click. Aubri quickly ducked into the room, closing, and locking the door behind her, before looking around. On the couch in the living room area, the makeshift curtain-and-rope combination that she and Bastian used from days ago was still intact. Aubri released a breath she didn't realized she held and couldn't stop the corners of her lips from curling upwards briefly, knowing too well that it could help save her life right now.

I just need to get across there to Colin's balcony, and then get rid of the rope before Renee can see from below. She coached herself. *It's going to be okay, Aubri. I'm going to be okay.*

Gunshots resounded again from outside the balcony as Aubri picked up her makeshift rope. *What was going on out there? Was Renee…?*

She recalled the guns she saw in Renee's room and shuddered. *How many people does she plan to kill out there?*

She crawled over to the window, taking one peek through, and saw one of the guests get shot, clutching their stomach as they fell into the pool. Aubri noticed both Nick and Bastian huddled together behind a few tables, trying to hide from Renee's sight. Aubri paled, quickly ducking back into the room before Renee could see her from the pool area.

Would Bastian and Nick be okay? I hope they stay alive. She whispered a quick prayer under her breath as she looked at the makeshift rope in her hands, and then the space between both balconies.

The last two times she snuck onto anyone's balconies, she had Bastian to hold the other end of the rope to keep it secure. Now that he wasn't here to do that, she had to secure it to something else. She grabbed a heavy side table and wrapped one end of the rope around the central leg. She then wrapped the other end around a chair as best as she could, before throwing the chair end towards Colin's balcony.

The chair almost missed the balcony entirely, but it latched onto the edge of the balcony railing and held fast. Aubri knew this wasn't the best scenario, and if it didn't work, it might fall apart.

Then again, better to die trying to get away from Renee, rather than falling to Renee herself.

She took a deep breath and made her way across the rope as fast as she could. The sounds of gunshots and screams continued resounding in her ears from below, and it only hastened her climbing. She made it to the other side, but barely; as she scampered onto Colin's balcony, she heard the chair snap from the earlier strain of holding the rope and her own weight. The section of rope tied to the chair descended until it did nothing but hang from her own balcony.

Aubri could only hope Renee hadn't seen it. Gunshots and screams continued to resonate, but they seemed fainter, now. Had Renee gone inside the building? Was she ascending the floors right now?

Either way, Aubri knew she had to hide quickly. Heading into Colin's room, she nearly tripped over the bedroom's night table as she looked around. Where could she hide, in this room? The closet? The bathroom? Aubri headed outside the bedroom and towards the living area, looking for a good hiding spot. If Renee didn't suspect she was in here, she'd be safe until the police arrived or until someone else came to help. Right?

Footsteps from outside made Aubri freeze on the spot, trying not to make too much noise. Even if she was hiding in Colin's room, she knew that if Renee heard her from outside, hiding in here wasn't worth the effort she made to get here.

"Aubri." Aubri stilled herself as she heard Renee call from outside. *"Where are you? Did you go to your room?"*

Aubri said nothing. She heard a snap of wood from outside, and then footsteps.

Renee's already investigating one of the rooms. My own, first?

She was suddenly glad she escaped. But then she swallowed, remembering how the makeshift rope and chair hung off Bastian's balcony. If Renee investigated Bastian's room, she might see those things. *What if she realizes I went into Colin's room?*

She had to hide. If Renee found her, then…

But that was when she heard Renee knocking on the door. Colin's door.

And Aubri was right inside Colin's suite.

She knows.

I'm dead.

CHAPTER 15

"Are you going to come out, Aubri?"

Aubri didn't say a word as she heard Renee's voice. If Renee had her cornered, Aubri knew she wasn't going down without a fight. She approached the dining table as quietly as she could and grabbed the nearest chair. It wasn't much of a weapon compared to guns, but at least it was something.

That was when the door suddenly burst open. Renee stood there, smiling at her, and Aubri did her best not to gag at the scent of the blood as Renee spoke too-cheerily.

"Hi, Aubri."

Renee was covered in blood, head to toe. It was something out of the movie Carrie, but not quite as blood-soaked…yet. There was enough that it soaked into her dress, her shoes, and some of it even dripped down her face. She seemed unfazed by her whole appearance, despite the circumstances that led to it.

"What did you do?" Aubri rasped, taking several steps back. She knew it was a useless question but stalling for time was the best she could do at this point! If the police came early, maybe they could come up here and stop Renee from killing her. The more she kept stalling the villain, the less likely she was to die – at least, that was what she remembered reading in the mystery novels.

Hopefully the same knowledge of mystery novels she had now could save her life.

Renee coolly smiled back at her as she walked into the room. "I killed everyone I could find, Aubri, so we could be alone together."

Aubri found herself backing up against the closest table. "Stay back." She whispered. *"Please."*

Renee shook her head, took a step closer. "Do you think I'd honestly rig the contest to make sure you and Colin got here, *only* so I could just watch you have fun on your own? I've had people take enough photos of you for that."

"Why did you do it? Why could you kill Colin?" Aubri wasn't sure what to do at this point, but *maybe* if she kept Renee talking, she could buy herself an opportunity to escape, at some point. Maybe lock Renee into this room, or disarm her, just *something.* Talking was the best distraction she had, and thankfully, she knew too well from both their time at this resort and during their past time dating each other that Renee loved to talk.

And besides, Aubri thought, *many murder mystery protagonists keep the true killer talking, to distract them from killing them. To buy themselves time until help arrives.*

She just hoped that this trick worked right now.

"I had to, Aubri. I had no other choice." Renee shrugged, looking down at the guns in both hands. She pulled the trigger of one of them to test it, but she scoffed as nothing sounded, tossing it aside. "Mommy dearest was *so* nice to give me the opportunity, after making a deal with the hotel manager, to invite me here after I found out both you *and* Colin, were coming over to this island…I was always her favourite daughter, after all." A smirk laced Renee's otherwise cold expression.

"So, it's true?" Aubri breathed, and she felt her hands shake her sides. "What Nessandra told me – your mom got her to rig the contest?"

"That bitch better do so if she wanted to keep her job." Renee's nose wrinkled at hearing Nessandra's name. "Other than that, it wasn't hard to find out about you and Colin, given the whole messy breakup and how you mentioned it on social media. It *did* take me a while to figure out that Bastian had past connections with you, though, given that he was the *only* random winner out of all of us. Both of you kept things *so* private that I might've missed him entirely as a new target."

A new target? Aubri felt her skin grow cold. *Is she...really going to kill Bastian, then?*

Renee continued speaking, a small smile appearing on her face. "But a few things gave it away, other than just you previously telling me about your history with him, that morning after Colin's death. I already knew about it the night before you told me back when I played the crybaby rich girl that wanted to just go home."

She held up her phone, and Aubri saw a familiar picture from her own social media profile. It was the same picture that Aubri took and posted of her and Bastian's hands laced together, their drinks shown at the edges of the photo. The caption read, *"Saw a friend today. It's nice to see him here."*

Aubri wished she hadn't posted that photo the first night she was at the resort, now.

"Wasn't hard to put two and two together. I saw him a few moments earlier, and I tried to kill him, *but* he ran away with that bartender friend." Renee shrugged, putting her phone away. "Haven't found him yet, unfortunately, but I'll kill him and his boytoy soon enough." Her brows furrowed, and she shook her head. "I assume he's been helping you with trying to investigate me, too, right? Can't leave out killing a crucial witness like him."

She hasn't found him and Nick yet, despite shooting up this place? That means...They're still alive. Aubri swallowed. Bastian was somewhere else, probably talking to the hotel management. Or maybe Bastian found the corpses of the hotel staff by now. Maybe he was hiding with Nick somewhere, hoping the police came a *lot* sooner than half an hour from now. Who knows? *At least they're safe for now.*

A chilling thought ran through her head immediately

afterwards. *What if he comes back up here, to check on me and make sure I'm safe? What if he walks in on me and Renee? What then?*

She had to do something. If Bastian came back alone *right now*, Renee would kill him. She had to find a way to get Renee away from her without risking anyone else's safety! Knock her out or something, perhaps? Her eyes gazed down at the chair she grasped in her hands, and then up at Aubri.

"There wasn't any point of you killing him, Renee!" Aubri burst out, looking Renee in the eyes. "He's my *ex*. There was no way I'm going back to him!"

Renee shrugged, but Aubri noticed her grip on the gun tighten. "I couldn't let things go to chance like that, Aubri! Men like him are asses anyway – you heard how he called you a *slut* on top of everything else! I did you a favor, getting rid of him!"

Aubri's brows furrowed at this. Sure, Colin wasn't the best person, but... "And murdering him was the best solution you could honestly think of, to make me get back together with you?!"

"I was hoping to keep it all covered up!" Renee's voice rose to a shriek, and Aubri found herself stepping back once. Renee's gaze turned to a glare, and she pointed the gun at her as she continued talking, arms shaking. "But *you* uncovered all the tracks before I could do enough to stop it. I did my best to frame it as an accident by pushing him over the balcony, pretended to play the scared girl who *didn't want to die,* but while I was doing so, I realized I that made one mistake: leaving my scarf at the scene of the crime. I should've taken it back after Colin grabbed it off my neck." Renee huffed, shaking her head, before snapping, "And then I also realized quickly that you broke into *my* room! I'd only just returned when I noticed that my balcony doors were left open."

Shit. Aubri knew she forgot to do *something* while leaving Renee's room, earlier. *So much for keeping my tracks covered.*

"And then there's Bastian," Renee continued, "Who decided to dig up my criminal record behind my back. I overheard both of you yelling at each other about it through the hotel room doors, that morning."

The case of the former ex-girlfriend Renee had, putting a restraining order on her due to assault? Aubri knew she had to keep Renee distracted still – could bringing up that past case help? "You would've killed her too, right? Your ex-girlfriend? Aria Hawthorn?"

Aubri watched Renee's nostrils flare at that, brows furrowing. "You should've seen how *cute* she was, Aubri. She looked *just* like you. It's a shame I couldn't get her to be with me." Her grip tightened on the gun, and Aubri swallowed as Renee put a finger on the trigger. "Her personality is nothing like yours, anyway. She didn't have the same fire. Too timid. *Weak.*"

Aubri wasn't sure whether she should feel sick about Renee comparing her to another ex-girlfriend, but it made her feel sick despite all of it. Renee took another step, then another towards her.

"I'm not going to kill you, Aubri – I don't need to if you just choose to come back to me." Renee's voice lowered to that familiar, honeyed tone she held, a sweet smile taking over her previously angered expression. "Why'd I do that to the woman I love, after all? All you must do is come back, Aubri. We can make this *right!* The police don't know anything. And *I'm* the daughter of this island's owner. We can easily make up a story. Right? I'll even spare Bastian and his boyfriend if they stay silent too, if you really want that."

It would be the easy option to give in. She couldn't deny that she still missed Renee. Even now, she wished that they were still dating, at times. They had been good to each other back in high school, getting into various shenanigans and having such a good time. But the fact that her ex killed another one of her exes, and then assaulted one of *her* own exes? And now she pulled off this massacre? Compared her to someone else she stalked? That crossed too many lines to Aubri at this point.

She looked into Renee's eyes, and shook her head once, before speaking. "No."

She saw Renee's eyes flash. *"What?"*

"You heard me, Renee." Aubri wasn't sure if she ever heard herself sound this angry before. Her jaw tensed as she stared down her ex-girlfriend, taking a step back. She held up the chair in her hands, pointing it at Renee. It wasn't the best weapon, especially since Renee still had one gun on hand, but at least it was something. "Get out of here, Renee. I don't want you back, *ever*. And you're not going to *make* me come back to you, no matter how many people you kill."

Renee stared at her, eyes widening. For a moment, Aubri thought that Renee might collapse and start crying. She could already see the tears welling up in the corners of her eyes, and Aubri felt bad for her, knowing too well that she broke her heart all over again.

However, it faded instantly as Renee burst into a scream, pointing the gun in her hand, and pulling the, only for her to find out that it was empty. Another snarl left her as she threw the gun aside, before flinging herself at Aubri. Aubri swung the chair, and it hit Renee in the upper torso, sending her sprawling onto the ground. Aubri ran for the bedroom, doing her best to slam the door shut and lock it as fast as she could, before pushing a desk up against the door in the attempt to keep it closed. She heard banging on the door, Renee screaming for her to open it, and she knew she had no time to waste.

"Shame I can't just *shoot* you, Aubri!" Aubri heard Renee scream from outside the door. "Shame I wasted all the fuckin' bullets on everyone in our way! But it's all worth it for *you*, darling! *Come back here!*"

She looked out the nearby door leading to the balcony. She noticed police officers, or security guards, approaching the resort's entrance, running in as fast as she could.

"Help me!" Aubri screamed. Some of the police seemed to look up, but most didn't notice as she tried to wave to them to get their attention. "Help me, *please!*"

The police mostly continued their way into the hotel building, and that was when it hit Aubri: The police were in the hotel lobby right now. Was there anyone else alive down in the lobby, other than the police? Maybe a few surviving staff? Could she call for help and alert the police to get up here, so they could arrest Renee and get this over with!? It was worth a shot, right?

Aubri rushed to the phone by her bed, before dialing the number for the front desk as she picked it up. The phone buzzed, then someone answered. Aubri's heart skipped a beat at hearing the front desk's staff person's voice. *Someone's still alive down there.* *"C-Calloway Resort's main desk speaking. I-if this is about the killer, the police have just arrived minutes ago and..."*

The police just arrived? Aubri's heart skipped another beat. This was her chance to get help – before it was too late!

"Please, help me!" Aubri yelled into the phone. She heard wood splinter behind her, and a gasp left her, a shudder running up her spine. *She broke through already!?* "Renee is trying to kill me!"

"Renee?"

"The other winner, yes! Please, help me! I'm on the top floor, room 701. Get the police up here—!"

Before she could hear the operator respond, Aubri felt the phone get ripped out of her hands before it was smashed against the wall. Aubri backed away in time to see Renee unplug the phone entirely, before picking up the entire machine and throwing it against the wall again, smashing it into countless pieces.

Aubri crawled over the bed, rolling over it entirely so she could make some distance between herself and Renee, but Renee easily caught up to her as she ran around the bed to catch up to her as Aubri tried standing fully. She felt Renee wrap an arm around her torso, and she screamed and kicked, flailing as hard as she could to try to get out of her iron grip. However, Renee was stronger than she hoped, despite the resistance.

"Stay still." Renee growled. Aubri stilled herself as she felt something cold and metallic against her throat. *A knife?* "Or else you're going to bleed open."

"Renee," Aubri managed, trying to keep her voice audible enough for the other to hear, "Please. *Don't* do this."

She felt her own heart beat a bit faster, and she heard Renee inhale deeply, before sighing once more.

"I don't know." She heard Renee chuckle, after a moment. "You always make this so difficult, Aubri. *You're* the one that made us break up in the first place. I'm not going to lose you now – not after all we've gone through!"

That was when Aubri heard footsteps, and she looked up to see Bastian rush into the room, holding a broken wine bottle in one hand as if it were a weapon. He looked a bit battered, but he wasn't visibly bleeding, and he was alive. His shocked, wide eyes narrowed instantly as he faced Renee and Aubri, pointing the broken bottle at them.

"Get away from her, Renee." A growl left his throat, shoulders tensing as he kept the sharp end of the bottle pointed. Aubri wasn't sure if she'd ever seen Bastian so angry before. He'd always been gentle and good to her. Firm, sure, when they argued, but he'd never sounded so rough until now.

"Bastian," Aubri whispered, but she felt Renee tug her closer against her as she laughed, Aubri seeing Renee's pearly whites flashing in her smile.

"Why should I?" Renee quipped, a low laugh leaving her. Aubri still felt the blade against her neck, but it wasn't pressed as hard against her throat anymore. "Because she's your former sugar baby?"

Bastian gritted his teeth, still holding the broken wine

bottle in his hand. "Because she's my *friend and fellow classmate.*"

Renee kept the knife against Aubri's neck. Aubri knew if she moved right now, Renee would probably kill her. Hell, she'd probably kill Bastian, too, now that he was here. How could they stop her?

She felt the cool breeze against her ankles, and she paused, looking towards the open doors of the balcony. Maybe she could lock Renee in the balcony area? She just had to get out of her grasp first…But *how?* Aubri had an idea, but it was a risky one. However, it was either this, or death. And frankly, she didn't want herself or Bastian to die.

"Give it up, Renee." Aubri whispered, glaring towards her as best as she could despite Renee still restraining her. "I'm not yours."

"You *will* be." Renee snapped back. "Or maybe I should just kill your friend first! He won't be in the way. I won't have to think of him fucking you, then."

"We never went that far in that relationship." Bastian clarified, and Aubri looked back towards him to see him raise a brow. "Nor do I intend that in the future. I *am* gay, if you didn't know until now, despite my obvious flirting with the cute bartender I adore and protected from you just earlier."

"Liar." Renee spat back, but Aubri felt Renee's grip on her loosen just slightly, the knife away from her neck. "You're lying, aren't you!?"

"I'm not lying when I say I'm her friend. But" He gestured to Renee and Aubri, "you certainly haven't done a good job of trying to woo her, what with threatening her life, murdering a whole bunch of people and pressuring her to get back together with you, on top of that."

Renee let go of Aubri, pushing her to the left, against the wall, before lunging at Bastian with the knife. Bastian swung his own glass bottle, and Aubri heard it shatter as it hit Renee in the head. Renee stumbled, missing her attempted stabbing of Bastian completely as she went off-balance, but Bastian quickly did his best to try to knock the knife of her hands, grabbing her from behind. However, Renee regained her balance and started grappling with him, elbowing him to get out of his grip and forcing him to grapple with her in hopes of avoiding injury.

Aubri's gaze darted towards the open balcony. The doors leading to it could be locked shut, right? Then…

"Bastian!" Aubri called to him, getting up as fast as she could. "We can lock her in the balcony area! Get her over here!"

"Are you sure?" Bastian yelped back, as he and Renee grappled with each other. "Is there enough space!?"

"Yeah! Hurry!"

Aubri dashed out of the way as Bastian continued grappling with Renee, shoving her closer to the balcony area as best as he could. They were close enough that with one hard shove, Bastian could probably get Renee off him and make her stumble into the balcony area.

Just as Bastian was about to do just that, however, Renee recovered enough to punch him in the face, sending Bastian stumbling back and hitting the floor. Aubri herself moved ahead to try to shove Renee into the balcony space, but that was when Renee grabbed her wrist, pulling her towards the balcony with her.

"*No!*" Aubri wasn't sure if it was her or Renee screaming, but she managed to pull her wrist out of Renee's grasp in one quick motion, before punching her in the face with her other hand. Renee gasped, staggering back against the balcony's railing, but the force of her stumble was enough for her to lean over the railing just enough so that she'd flip over completely and fall.

…At least, she *would* fall if Aubri didn't do a thing to stop her. Without thinking, Aubri ran forwards, grabbing at Renee, and managed to grab her wrist. She heard a 'crack' from the other's wrist due to the momentum of the fall, on top of twisting Renee's wrist when trying to catch her. A pained yelp left Renee, and Aubri looked down to see Renee gasping, her eyes streaked with tears.

"Help me," Aubri heard Renee plead, whimpering, "Please. *Please* don't drop me!"

Aubri swallowed. She knew she could let go, and let Renee fall, likely leading to death. But what would that mean? Was she no better than her if that was the case?

She shook her head lightly. Renee might've tried to kill her and Bastian, but Aubri wasn't a killer herself. She couldn't let her die. Maybe Renee came to her senses now, given what was going on. She took a deep breath, before looking Renee in the eyes.

"Just hold on, okay? I'm gonna pull you up. Just give me a few moments!"

Another little sob left Renee, and guilt flooded Aubri's chest at hearing her plea. "P-please, hurry!"

"What are you doing!?" Aubri heard Bastian yell from just inside the bedroom. "Aubri, she's literally trying to kill us!"

"I can't just kill *her!*" Aubri turned her head to yell back at him. "I'm not a murderer!"

"She tried to kill us first!" Bastian's brows furrowed as he yelled back. "It's practically self defense if she dies because of either of us at this point! Murder mysteries are a sucker for that plot point!"

Aubri turned her head back towards Renee, just in time to see Renee snarl and take out another, smaller, knife from the pocket of her shorts, before stabbing at Aubri.

Aubri instinctively let go of her hand—and *immediately* regretted it as Renee's gaze distorted into horror, as she began falling. Renee flailed in the air, waving her arms, trying to grab onto the sides of the building, but she was falling too fast to snag onto anything or anyone for help.

"Renee!"

Aubri felt Bastian's strong arms wrap around her waist, pulling her back hard as Renee's hand slipped out of hers.

"Aubri!"

"Let go of me, Bastian!" Aubri tried to pull out of his grasp, and he did. She ran over to the balcony—

Just in time to hear a massive *crunch* as Renee hit the pool deck, her entire body slumping into a bloody heap. Aubri had to look away as it hit her—her ex-girlfriend was dead. Gone.

It was all over.

"Aubri?"

She looked up to see Bastian. He looked shaken, having heard Renee's landing only moments ago, and he swallowed as he looked Aubri in the eye. Aubri felt tears prick at the corners of her eyes before she threw herself into his arms. Memories of Renee danced in her mind, of how she once loved her, how they dated back in high school. The warm kisses. Her honeyed words.

And only a few moments ago, Renee tried to kill her.

Aubri swallowed, trying to blink tears out of her eyes, but she knew that even though the killing might just be over, what she felt right now about Renee wouldn't leave her. Not for a long, long time.

CHAPTER 16

The police burst into the room only moments after Renee's fall to her death. Bastian and Aubri, shaken from earlier but knowing too well about the whole situation, explained everything to them, even handing over the USB that Aubri copied Renee's files onto to the police as evidence.

Hours later, after the police gathered the survivors and attended to them, as well as examining the evidence and finding more of it in Renee's room, it was clear that Aubri wouldn't be charged for what happened, neither would Bastian, due to self-defence reasons. However, it was also clear that this vacation was over, and none of the guests wanted to stay any longer at this resort.

Nessandra, who miraculously survived Renee's earlier assault due to being non-fatally shot and thanks to the police giving her medical assistance, offered to keep in touch and give both Bastian and Aubri another free week of vacation at the resort without any drama, to make up for the whole mess. Nessandra was completely distraught over the whole affair; after all, she would have to explain to the owner that her own daughter, Renee, was the one that initially murdered Colin, *and* massacred majority of the guests while trying to kill Aubri and Bastian. Despite Nessandra's apologies and generous offer, however, Aubri wasn't sure if she ever wanted to come back to this place.

Right now, she was just relieved that Nessandra managed to book her and Bastian (as well as the surviving guests at the resort) a plane back home. It wasn't a luxurious first class (it was business class, but still not as great), but it was something. And Aubri wanted nothing to do with this resort anymore. At least, for now.

Aubri knew that she wanted nothing to do with Renee anymore, too.

She and Bastian coincidentally had seats beside each other on the plane going home, and Aubri sighed as she looked out the window, watching the island they left shrinking the distance. Who ever thought a vacation could end on such a tragic note?

"Are you okay?"

She looked towards Bastian, who just put down an empty can of juice. Aubri simply nodded, before picking up her own can of juice and taking a few sips.

"I'll be okay." She managed. "Probably not for a while."

"That's fair." He faltered, then managed, "Sorry. For not doing more to help."

"You did a lot to help, Bastian." She elbowed him slightly with her left arm. "It's me. *I* should've realized that Renee was the killer. Should've done the research like you did and accepted the truth a lot sooner. Also, you saved your bartender friend's life, so that's something."

A chuckle left him as he held up a small note reading *"Call Me"* with a number attached. "Nick certainly was flattered, yes, but *you* found the actual evidence." He pointed out. "I wasn't the one that snuck into her room and found all the murder plans for Colin on her laptop before copying it onto a USB and sneaked out."

"But you almost died." Aubri paused, before looking him in the eye. "What happened out there with you and Nick, exactly?"

"I got to Nick at the bar. He just finished his shift when Renee started shooting everyone she could see." He admitted. "We got across the pool area and into the building where the bar was – remember when Nick escorted us out that back door to the elevators? That's how I made it all the way up to your floor. After I made Nick hide in another closet close to the main lobby where the police could find him, I went straight to your room to check on you and make sure you were okay."

"And where did you get the broken wine bottle from?"

He shrugged, a light grin playing on his face. "Picked it up from the bar while hiding with Nick. I figured it was a better weapon than nothing."

"You better be glad she ran out of bullets by the time you arrived." She swallowed, shaking her head. "Otherwise..."

A sigh left him as he leaned back in his seat, closing his eyes briefly. "I know. It wouldn't have ended well. Let's not imagine that any longer, alright?"

Silence momentarily fell between them. What they went through was nothing short of terrifying, and Aubri knew that the what-ifs and possible bad endings from that incident would haunt her for a while. She paused, before asking, "Do you think she would have killed both of us? If she overpowered us, that is?"

"I don't know, and I don't think I *want* to know." Bastian looked down, then up at Aubri. "So...what now? Other than getting home and trying to forget about all of this?"

"Well," Aubri paused, before speaking again, her eyes meeting his, "I was thinking...maybe it might be a good idea to stick with you, for a bit?"

"Me?" he stared back at her, brows furrowing. "Why?"

She shrugged, before offering him the best smile she could. "You're my friend, obviously. And I trust you. And I don't think I want to date anymore, for a long time, but I don't want to be alone, either."

"Were you living by yourself before this?" He asked, tilting his head to the side.

"Yeah. I don't think I could feel safe being alone, though. Not after all," She gestured in the general direction of the island with a hand, "That."

"Well..." Bastian paused, taking a deep breath. He leaned back in his seat, a sigh leaving him. "I live in an apartment in Toronto. How far are you from there?"

"I'm in London, right now." He stared at her, before she laughed. "London, *Ontario* that is, not England. But I can make the trip to Toronto on a bus or train, and. I'm paying for my own ticket before you ask. I've got more than enough money from work to pay for it."

A sheepish grin spread across Bastian's face. "And we split rent?"

She couldn't help but smile at that. "We'll see how soon I get work-related stuff in order. I'm sure my boss wouldn't mind me working from home, given what I do, but I'll probably get reduced hours or something. We'll figure it out."

"We will." He shrugged. "If we can figure out who's a murderer, I'm sure you and job-related work won't be so difficult."

A laugh left her. "That's fair."

For once, she could focus on herself; her and her friend, of course. And it was an odd arrangement, to be together as friends again and living in the same place, especially considering their past shared history. But right now, that was just what Aubri needed – A safe place with someone she could trust, and far, far away from dating life.

She'd figure it out in time.

She knew both would.

AFTERWORD

Thank you for reading "Winner Takes All!" I hope that you enjoyed reading the first of the *Harlow Mystery* series.

Please consider leaving a review! It helps with making this book better-known to new readers. If you want to check out more of me and my work, you can find me at:

Website:
https://clarislam.ca

Email newsletter:
https://buttondown.com/clarislamauthor

Bluesky:
https://bsky.app/profile/clarislamauthor.bsky.social

Facebook:
https://www.facebook.com/ClarisLamAuthor

Instagram:
https://www.instagram.com/clarislamauthor/
Tumblr:
https://clarislam.tumblr.com/

Bookbub:
https://www.bookbub.com/profile/claris-lam

Goodreads:
https://www.goodreads.com/author/
show/22277014.Claris_Lam

ABOUT THE AUTHOR

Claris Lam

Claris Lam (she/her) writes poetry and fiction to inspire readers with hope, perseverance, creativity, and happy endings.

Claris' short fiction and poetry has been published in collections and projects. She has self-published a murder mystery series entitled the Harlow Mystery series. Her latest novel, Bloody Fantasia, was published in June 2024. She is currently writing several novels and poetry chapbooks. Learn more about her work at https://clarislam.ca.

BOOKS IN THIS SERIES

Harlow Mystery

Engagement To Die For

"Engagement To Die For" brings family reunions, dark secrets and histories revealed, and more murder where "Winner Takes All" left off!

After everything Aubri went through at the resort, the last thing Aubri needs is more drama. However, meeting her previously-unknown twin sister for the first time, and attending her mother's engagement party, results in yet another murder.

Due to the remote area of this crime, the police won't be able to make it for a few days. Aubri realizes that she, along with her friends and her sister, must take up the mantle themselves to solve the case or risk being new victims again.

Bloody Fantasia

The finale to the Harlow Mystery series is finally here!

In "Bloody Fantasia," Aubri Harlow and her friends believe that their days of investigating murders are over. However, when Aubri's sister, Aria, moves into her new music school, the Da Capo Institution, the school's acting president suddenly dies during the welcoming ceremonies.

However, the acting president's death is far from the first murder committed on campus. A string of past murders haunt the school's reputation and its students. It doesn't take long before new corpses start piling up, and Aubri, Aria, and their friends realize they must take up the mystery-solving mantle once more and find out who the murderer is.

Will they figure out the person responsible for causing these new tragedies, or will they become part of its bloody history? Find out by reading "Bloody Fantasia!"